# CREATURE
## OF HABIT

# CREATURE
## OF HABIT

KIERAN RIVIERE

# CREATURE OF HABIT

iUniverse books may be ordered through booksellers or by contacting:

iUniverse
1663 Liberty Drive
Bloomington, IN 47403
www.iuniverse.com
844-349-9409

ISBN: 978-1-6632-3119-2 (sc)
ISBN: 978-1-6632-3120-8 (e)

Library of Congress Control Number: 2021922237

Print information available on the last page.

iUniverse rev. date:  11/19/2021

# CHAPTER 1

With his parents' blessing, Sire was ready to embark on his journey to the Big Apple. He was a man without a plan, but his father had given him thirty thousand dollars to start off with. The twelve-hour flight from Ramon International Airport in Israel seemed endless, but Sire had brought along an old mp3 player to help pass the time. He finally landed at John F. Kennedy International Airport after several naps. Sire could not believe it. He was finally in New York, a place he had longed to visit for what seemed like his entire life. After clearing customs, he went to the appropriate carousel to look for his luggage. Soon after grabbing his bag from the carousel, Sire was quickly accosted by a Jamaican taxi driver. "Taxi!" he shouted, while pointing at Sire. "Where you going sir?" With no particular destination in mind, Sire asked the taxi driver to take him to the nearest hotel. It did not take long for the driver to realize that Sire was unfamiliar with the city. He took Sire to a random hotel in downtown Manhattan and charged him a hundred and twenty dollars for what was normally a sixty-dollar ride. This first encounter upon his arrival gave Sire his first taste of the "New York Hustle."

He checked in at the Hampton Inn Hotel at a rate of nearly two hundred dollars per night. It would become his home for the months ahead. Lacking any formal plan, Sire would venture out into the city on foot; each day going a bit further than the last. He had developed a passion for music while living in Israel and had hoped to become a successful artist one day. For the time being, however, he was content with acquiring a decent job until he figured out how he would achieve his goal. Navigating through the crowded streets of Manhattan can be a task for even the most seasoned New Yorkers. For Sire, it felt like he was walking through a Nigerian Day parade, but with less Nigerians and less costumes. One afternoon, Sire wandered as far as Central Park, where he met a Senegalese man who was handing out flyers for a bus tour around the city. He wore a bright yellow polo t-shirt and handed Sire a flyer that read "Big Bus Tours." Even if he did not know the man, Sire was pleased to have met another African like himself. He had been longing to meet up with someone from Nigeria, or any other African country. Most of the people Sire came across while staying at the hotel were either American or European tourists. After a brief conversation, Sire gave the man his phone number and told him to call anytime there was an opening at his job, then made his way back to the hotel.

Sire had been staying at the Hampton Inn Hotel for approximately six months. One afternoon, while sitting at a café, he checked his account and realized that he had spent nearly two thirds of his money on hotel fees and food. With no source of income, it became obvious that he could not afford to stay at the hotel much longer. He needed to find a job soon, or he would be forced to live on the street. Sire remembered an American friend he had back in Israel by the name of Kent, who had gone to the same school as him. Kent grew up in New York but moved to Israel with his mother after his father died. Without wasting time, he went looking for Kent on Facebook, to see if Kent would be able to help him to find a cheaper place to live. Facebook was fairly new around this time. Luckily, Sire and Kent had mutual friends, so he was not very hard to find. When Kent found out that Sire had been staying in a Manhattan hotel for six months, he asked Sire if he was crazy. "You need to move out of there ASAP," he said, "go look for a room in Brooklyn or Queens."

The following day, instead of wandering around aimlessly in the bustling streets of Manhattan, Sire decided to heed Kent's advice and went searching for a room to rent. As he approached the subway station nearest to the hotel, he remembered the movie "Coming to America," and decided that he would try visiting Queens first, like Eddie Murphy. Sire was amazed to see that life underground was just as lively as life above ground. Even the subway rats were boisterous, the way they scurried across the platform as if they were crossing a busy street. He could barely understand the subway map, but the clerk in the metro card booth told him where to stand for the Queens-bound trains. When the train stopped at Sutphin Boulevard, Sire noticed a lot of people getting off, so he figured that it would be a good place to start. The first thing Sire noticed was that Queens was vastly different from Manhattan. The sidewalks were less crowded and there were fewer skyscrapers. The intermittent honking came from the dollar-vans and gypsy cabs driving up and down the avenues, rather than the infamous yellow taxis. He walked past a Guyanese market with a plethora of fruits in the front, which gave him a euphoric feeling. It was the middle of July, and the sun was extremely hot that day. However, Sire was not hindered by the heat; his dark skin was accustomed to extreme weather conditions from growing up in Nigeria. He purchased a bottle of water from a man standing near a street corner with a cooler. He did not have the slightest clue where to begin looking for a place to stay. After walking around for some time, Sire noticed a flyer on a light post advertising a room for rent. He dialed the number on the flyer and a lady with a Spanish accent answered. With some broken English, and a few Spanish words mixed in, she explained that she had a room available for rent on the second floor of her house. The going price was one hundred and fifty dollars weekly. Sire was flabbergasted. He was paying almost ten times more at the hotel. He wrote down the address, flagged own a black gypsy cab, and made his way to her home.

When he arrived at the address, Sire called the lady to tell her that he was outside. It was a two-story house, painted in white, with a front yard and a fence that reached up to Sire's waist. Looking around, he noticed that most of the homes on that street had the same blueprint. The lady opened the front door and Sire was surprised to see that she was much shorter than he had imagined. *People never really looked how they sounded over the phone*, he thought. Sire was only a little over five feet in height, but he felt like a giant standing next to his future landlady. Her name was Laura, she was Colombian-born and lived alone with her two cats. Since her kids moved out and started families of their own, she decided to rent out the rooms that were left vacant. She greeted Sire with a smile and showed him the way to the room that was available. Upon entering the house, Sire noticed two doors. There was one that led to the steps to the second floor and the other door led to the first-floor apartment where Laura stayed. There were two bedrooms upstairs. One was vacant and the other was occupied by a girl named Sufiah, who was at work at the time. There was also a kitchen and a bathroom, which seemed to be well kept and orderly. Sire was impressed and told Laura that he would take the room. He returned to the Hampton Inn hotel and began packing his clothes so that he could move out the following day.

It did not take long for Sire to acclimate to his new home in Queens. He became acquainted with his new roommate Sufiah, and they gradually developed a friendship. Sufiah was born and raised in Pakistan and had moved to New York with her parents during her teenage years. She was a few years older than Sire, who had just turned twenty at the time. She had a light brown complexion with long silky hair. She worked Monday through Saturday, so Sire only saw her in the evenings and on Sundays. Most of Sufiah's leisure time was spent with her boyfriend Sam, who would visit her a few times a week. A Brazil-born man, Sam looked like he could be Sufiah's brother. They had the same complexion and shared similar facial features. Sire's relationship with Sam was barely cordial. The two hardly spoke, other than a greeting or a head nod every now and then. However, it was not Sam's lack of words that kept Sire at a distance, rather it was his actions. Anytime Sufiah and Sire were alone in the kitchen, even for a short moment, Sam would pop up with no real purpose other than to caress Sufiah in front of Sire. After it happened a fifth time, Sire decided to avoid the kitchen entirely anytime Sam was at the apartment. When Sam was not around, Sire and Sufiah would sit outside on the stoop and talk about life's affairs. Sufiah was an avid smoker and one day she offered Sire his first cigarette which he accepted. From that day, Sire began smoking with Sufiah occasionally, until it became a habit. Before long, he was buying his own packs.

One evening, while talking on the stoop, Sire mentioned to Sufiah that he was looking for work. By then, he had exceeded the amount of time that he was allowed to stay in the country. He was officially an illegal immigrant. Although his living expenses had decreased greatly since moving to Queens, Sire knew that he had to find a job soon, or risk becoming homeless. He remembered his father's words and suddenly, it made sense why his father was initially against him coming to New York. He thought to himself, *maybe he knew how difficult life would be without anyone to depend on or how easily one can become homeless.* Lucky for Sire, the print shop where Sufiah worked needed an extra worker at the time. "I will speak to the owner tomorrow," she said, while putting a cigarette to her mouth. The following day, Sire was at home surfing the internet when Sufiah called. She had spoken to the owner, and he agreed for Sire to start the next day. Labor Day was around the corner, and they needed help fulfilling increased demand. Sire was quite pleased and grateful, but he was also nervous. It was his first job, and he did not know what to expect. He waited until Sufiah got in from work to discuss his new position. After speaking with Sufiah, he felt less worried. After all, it was only a print shop, he thought.

The following morning, Sire left the house together with Sufiah at around 9 a.m. The bus ride to Maspeth was approximately forty minutes with moderate traffic. Everyone was expected to be at work by 10 a.m. When they arrived at the printshop around a quarter to ten, they met the owner in the front of the shop pulling up the metal gates. His name was Miles. He was a tall, skinny Guyanese man with a few gold teeth that glistened in the sun when he smiled. Sufiah greeted Miles and proceeded to introduce him to Sire.

"This the guy?" Miles asked.

"Good morning sir," Sire said. "I wanted to thank you for giving me a job."

"You ever used a laser printer before?"

"No sir."

Sire looked at Sufiah perplexed. He wondered if she had told Miles that he was an experienced printer to increase his chances of getting the job. If that was the case, it seemed silly to him that Sufiah did not give him the heads up. This made them both look stupid, he thought. However, the lack of concern on her face seemed to indicate that all was well.

"Okay, no worries," Miles said. "I'll let Marlon teach you when he comes in. This guy is forever late."

All three of them entered the print shop after the gates were up. Sufiah showed Sire around the shop, then went to get started on her paperwork. She told him that Marlon would arrive at any minute to show him how to use the printers. Before long, a short dark-skinned man walked in. "This is my roommate I told you about Marlon," Sufiah said. Marlon introduced himself to Sire and went to the back of the print shop to put his lunch in the fridge. Miles had left the shop to fetch supplies, so Marlon went straight to Sire to get him started on his training. For a short man, Marlon had a noticeably loud voice, which projected across the print shop like an echo in a cave. He was born in Guyana, and although he had only spent the first twelve years of his life there, his strong Guyanese accent was indicative of someone who had only recently arrived in the United States. After only two days of training, Sire was able to operate the laser printing machine by himself. He had developed a friendship with Marlon and soon they were hanging out together on weekends. Marlon was an experienced DJ and he had been playing at parties and clubs for over ten years. As time went on, Sire became increasingly interested in becoming a DJ himself. Although his true passion was to become a singer, he saw the potential for making money in the DJ industry, so he welcomed the skills and knowledge.

As time went by, Sire's friendship with Sufiah began to dwindle. Sam was spending more time at the apartment than usual, and Sufiah began acting strangely towards Sire whenever he was around. It became apparent that Sam was trying to put a wedge between Sire and Sufiah. Sire tried his best to avoid the two. Even at work, he limited his communication with Sufiah to strictly matters of the business. Back at the apartment, Sam found every possible reason to pick a fight with Sire. One day, he told Sire that he was taking up too much space in the fridge. Sire avoided confrontation with Sam for as long as he could, until he finally reached his breaking point. An argument between the two nearly turned physical when Sire walked up to Sam to confront him. It became so intense that it woke his landlady out of her sleep. She and Sufiah tried desperately to keep the two from fighting and she had to threaten to call police for them to stop. The following day, Sire left for work earlier than usual. He waited until Sufiah left the shop on her lunch break to vent to Marlon about the situation at the apartment. "I need to find another place to stay," he said. "I didn't come all the way to New York just to end up in prison for something stupid." Marlon told Sire to relax, and that he might know someone who is renting a room across the street from his home in Brooklyn. He made a phone call and told Sire to come to Brooklyn with him after work so that they could see the room. The commute to Brooklyn seemed endless on the crowded J-train. When they arrived at Broadway Junction, Sire and Marlon decided to take a taxi instead of waiting for the L-train. Marlon lived in Brownsville for most of his life and knew the folks in the neighborhood quite well. Across the street from where he lived was an apartment building owned by a Jamaican widow with two kids. He had seen one of the tenants moving out the week before, so he contacted the lady to find out if the apartment was still vacant. The apartment was fully furnished and only costed Sire a couple hundred dollars more than what he was paying for his room in Queens. After seeing the apartment and meeting with the landlady, Sire decided to move in that same weekend.

In a matter of weeks, Sire had gotten used to his new neighborhood. He made a few friends around the area and even flirted with some of the girls. When he was not at work, he was hanging across the street at Marlon's. The house was owned by Marlon's mother, Miss Ingrid. She stayed upstairs, while Marlon stayed downstairs with his son Edward and his son's mother Deborah. Although they lived together, Marlon and Deborah were not on best of terms. Continuous arguments had driven the two to despise each other. Every time Sire heard the two arguing, he wondered how they got together in the first place. Deborah was quite tall for a woman, nearly twice Marlon's height, with breasts slightly larger than average. She had smooth dark skin, and her hair was usually worn in a ponytail, making her look a few years younger than her real age of thirty-one. To Sire, they were just an odd couple. Sire was rather pleased with the way things had been going for him. He had a job, a roof over his head, and a world of opportunities ahead of him. Things took a turn for the worst however, when the store owner Miles began to squander the profits from the print shop on his drug habits. Everyone had begun to suspect Miles' drug use after seeing drug paraphernalia left around the store by mistake. Eventually, he was no longer able to manage the shop's expenses and pay his workers, which ultimately led to the shop going out of business.

Soon after losing his job, Sire fell into a state of depression. He knew that as an illegal immigrant, it would be difficult for him to find another job. He had enough money in his account to pay rent for the next two months, but beyond that, he did not know how he was going to make it work. One afternoon, after listening to Sire voice his concerns, Marlon asked Miss Ingrid if Sire could stay with them until he found another job. Miss Ingrid welcomed Sire without the slightest hesitation. Sire was always well-mannered whenever he was over at Miss Ingrid's house, and one could argue that she treated him better than her own son. Miss Ingrid loved Marlon, but they also could not stand each other. She thought Marlon was lazy, while Marlon thought she was rapacious. Sire was grateful to Marlon and his mother for providing him with shelter while he was unemployed. He finished off his stay at his apartment and moved across the street at the end of the month.

Shortly after moving in, Sire observed Marlon's and Deborah's relationship begin to worsen. With more time on his hands, Marlon began to stalk Deborah and accuse her of sleeping with her co-workers. Sire usually heard the arguments from his room upstairs, but not once did he ever intervene. He was against interfering in couples' affairs unless they became physical. Eventually, the arguments began to dwindle after Marlon met a Jamaican girl at one of his weekend events. He began spending very little time at home and often slept over at the girl's house. Miss Ingrid, on the other hand, worked as a live-in nanny in Westchester and would only come home on weekends. Meanwhile, since Deborah was working, Sire spent most of his afternoons looking after Edward. Deborah was outwardly grateful to Sire for watching her son while she worked. Most nights after work, she would bring home liquor and food for Sire, as a gesture of thanks for his role in Edward's life. Sire had developed a good relationship with the kid. However, his depression continued to worsen. Despite not having to pay rent, the idea of not working drove him insane. He quickly developed a drinking habit while trying to cope with his depression. One late night, Sire was in the basement drinking heavily and listening to some music when he heard Deborah's footsteps upstairs. He decided that it was time for him to retire to his bedroom and started making his way up the steps. Deborah was coming down at the same time and her breast accidentally rubbed against Sire's chest as they passed each other in the narrow staircase.

Deborah had spent most of her life in St. Lucia where she was born and raised. Her father left St. Lucia when she entered high school and ended up in Maryland where he got married to an American woman. After he was fully naturalized, he filed for Deborah, who was his only child at the time. He eventually had two kids with his wife. After living in Maryland for a year, Deborah moved to New York where she stayed with an aunt and found a job at Home Depot. She met Marlon through a mutual friend at a backyard barbeque. Marlon was one of the DJs that day. He caught Deborah's attention with his vivacious character; especially when he was on the mike. Soon after, the two started dating and after three months she became pregnant with Edward. After learning that Deborah was pregnant, the relationship began to go downhill. Marlon was not working at the time, and he always assumed that Deborah was sleeping with other men. Despite their differences, they tried to make the relationship work for Edward's sake. But they seemed to have given up hope along the way.

Deborah could tell that Sire was mildly inebriated when she passed him on the staircase. She told him that he should sleep on the mattress in the living room where the air conditioner was, instead of his hot room upstairs. Anyone staying in New York in the summertime knew that a fan was ineffective against the heavy humid air on hot summer days. Sire gladly obliged and made his bed on the living room floor. The next morning, to Sire's surprise, he woke up to find Deborah lying asleep next to him. As strange as it was, he thought nothing of it because she was fully clothed in tights and a t-shirt. Nevertheless, during the day, Sire tried to make sense out of the odd scenario. He was sure that Deborah had an air-conditioner in her room, so it could not have been the heat. *Maybe she just wanted some company*, he thought, *because of Marlon's absence.* But that thought quickly faded from his mind. He could not imagine Deborah betraying Marlon like that, especially not with one of his closest friends. A few nights later, Sire had retired to his room early and fell asleep with his laptop on the bed next to him. Suddenly, he began to feel his briefs being pulled off his legs. He opened his eyes and saw Deborah standing over him naked. Before he could utter a word, she placed one of her breasts in his mouth. That night marked the beginning of a salacious secret under the roof of Miss Ingrid's house.

Solomon was eager to arrive home from work, to share the good news with his wife, Ekema. He had finally gotten appointed a diplomat, a position he had long anticipated. After working at the immigration office for thirteen years, Solomon had grown increasingly fed up with his role as a clerk. The mundanity of filing the same forms each day had begun to take its toll. One afternoon, as he was clearing his desk to go home, Solomon's boss told him that he was being considered for a diplomatic position by the foreign minister. The following day, he was asked to attend a training session, where the details of the position was explained. After several months of waiting, Solomon had begun to think that the position was given to someone else. *Maybe they had given it to some far cousin, or some family friend*, he thought. Nepotism was rather rampant in Nigeria, especially in small communities. Besides, it wasn't like he had any formal education in foreign affairs. Most of his acquired knowledge had come from years of on-the-job training. The long-awaited day had finally arrived, however. As he was about to shut his computer down, Solomon received an email from the foreign minister congratulating him on his achievement. He then packed up his work bag and headed off to his wife and kids to share the news.

When Solomon entered the house, he noticed Ekema setting the dining room table. Her white t-shirt was stained with seasoning. Wasting no time, Solomon cornered Ekema next to the dining table and proceeded to kiss her neck. "What has gotten into you today?" she asked, while enjoying the sensual greeting. Before Solomon could speak, the two were interrupted by their sons, Shelo and Sire. They heard when their father had entered the house and came down from their rooms to greet him. At the time, Shelo was seven, and a few inches taller than his brother Sire, who had just turned five. They could always tell when their father had entered the house by the sound of his footsteps. Solomon waited until everyone was seated at the table to share the news. Ekema was elated at the news of her husband's new position. The small family would have to move from their home in Taraba State Nigeria, to settle near the embassy in the capital city of Abuja. Ekema did not mind the relocation. A great part of her teenage life was spent in Abuja, where she attended school. The boys were excited about the move as well, despite having to leave their old school behind.

The family of four was just beginning to get accustomed to life in the city, when Ekema gave birth to her first daughter, Grace. The boys had started school and Solomon was becoming acclimated to his new role at the embassy. Ekema took care of the home and the children. She was a well-educated woman, but before she could begin her career in healthcare, she became pregnant with Shelo. Ekema and Solomon had met while she was still attending college. As soon as she graduated, Solomon decided that it was time to start his family. At the time, he had a steady job and could afford to support a family on his monthly salary. After laying eyes on Ekema for the first time at a cultural festival, Solomon was certain that she would be the woman that would share his last name. She wore an elegant purple dress which complemented her dark skin. Her natural hair illuminated her confidence and pride. Although she was a little shorter than average, her beauty made her stand out, like a rose among grass. Ekema was happy to stay home to take care of her baby and by the time Shelo was two, she became pregnant with Sire. As the years went by, she became accustomed to her role as the woman of the house, but she was still hopeful that one day, when the kids were old enough, she would venture out into the work force and finally begin her career.

One Friday afternoon, Sire was sitting in the school library waiting for Shelo to get out of his afternoon classes. They normally walked home together. The librarian had become accustomed to seeing Sire's face around the library from time to time. Her thick eyeglasses always looked like they were falling off her nose. While waiting, Sire began flipping through a magazine that was left on one of the tables. It happened to be a travel magazine. On one of the pages, there was a picture of the Statue of Liberty and on another, there was an aerial view of New York city in the nighttime. Sire was marveled by the sight of New York City's skyline. He flipped back to the page with the Statue of Liberty and heard it calling his name. On the third "Sire," he realized only that it was Shelo calling for him from down the corridor. He picked up his book bag and ran to meet him. That night, as Sire lay in his bed, his mind wandered back to those magazine pictures of New York. It left an indelible impression on his young memory.

Life in Abuja was splendid. Solomon was earning almost twice as much as what he was earning at his first job. The kids had gotten used to the commute to and from school on their own, while Ekema used the time at home to care for their youngest child. She was even able to maintain her vegetable garden which she had started at the back of the house. Before long, the small family welcomed two more boys in quick succession. They were now a family of seven, with four boys and one girl. Soon after his last son David was born, Solomon was transferred to a new post in Sao Tome and Principe, an island off the West coast of Africa. The family was soon on their way to start a new life on the peaceful island. Ekema was not too thrilled about the move but understood that relocation was part of her husband's role at the embassy. The kids, on the other hand, were excited about the relocation. Although they had made friends at their schools, they were intrigued by the idea of a new environment. Sire had the least friends. He was especially excited about the move, partially because he thought it would bring him closer to visiting New York.

Sao Tome and Principe was a new world to the family. The lifestyle was much different from what they were accustomed to in Abuja. With a population of approximately 150,000 people at the time, the island was mostly known for its exotic beaches and lustrous rainforests. Shelo and Sire did not immediately go back to school because they were not yet accustomed to the Portuguese language which was dominant on the island. That left them with a lot of free time to get into trouble and for chasing girls. At the time, Sire had just turned sixteen while Shelo had entered adulthood at eighteen. One afternoon, Sire accidentally walked in on Shelo while he was having his way with one of the girls from the village and threatened to spill the beans if he did not get his slice of the pie. The nineteen-year-old girl, a tall, skinny girl with long hair named Camila, agreed to meet up with Sire the following day after Shelo gave her the green light. Coincidentally, while Sire was about to get started, his younger sister Grace accidentally walked in on him and spoiled the show for him too.

After only two years of living in Sao Tome and Principe, it was time for the family to migrate again. Solomon was appointed to a temporary post in Germany, where the family stayed for a few months before getting stationed in Netanya Israel. They would spend the next few years there and the kids eventually returned to school. Ekema stayed home as always, while Solomon supported the family. When Sire had turned eighteen, he knew that at some point the family would have to move back to Nigeria, their home country. He decided instead that he would try to find his way to New York, the place where he had longed to visit for most of his life. He went on the internet one day and found some information on the process of acquiring a US visa. Ekema had noticed what he was doing, and Sire was able to convince her to apply for his younger siblings as well. Ekema was reluctant to mention anything to Solomon regarding the application, because of his harsh outlook on America and American customs. Throughout his life, the media had given Solomon a distorted view of America and he often spoke of having no interest in going there. One afternoon, Ekema shared the idea with her younger brother, Akin, who was staying with them at the time. Akin had only recently moved to Israel, where he lived with a friend of his near the capital. He was a little older than Sire and had no family of his own. One evening, he arrived home to find that his keys were not working anymore. There was an eviction notice plastered on the front door. His friend that he was sharing the apartment with had moved back to his parent's house, leaving Akin with nowhere to stay. Luckily, he had his older sister to depend on and she took him in until he could get back on his feet. After getting the idea from Ekema, Akin applied for his US visa a few days later and scheduled an appointment with the US embassy. Unfortunately, Akin was denied despite having high hopes. A week later, Ekema decided to apply for the younger kids, but they got denied as well. Sire was privy to all the visa talk that was going around, and he became doubtful when everyone else had gotten rejected. A few months had passed and all the talk around the house concerning America had subsided. One night, Sire dreamt that he was at the airport in Nigeria, waiting on an American Airlines flight. He woke up the next morning and decided to make an appointment to go to the US embassy the following week.

The morning of his appointment, Sire did not tell anyone where he was going. The commute to Jerusalem from Tel Aviv-Yafo was a tiresome one. He had to take two buses and a taxi. Upon arrival, the first thing Sire noticed was the two enormous flags hanging from the embassy building: one Israeli and the other American. There were people walking in and out of the building through what seemed to be the main entry point. Sire looked around and felt a bit underdressed. Everyone seemed to be in business attire, while he was dressed in long jeans pants and a plain black polo t-shirt. He pulled his appointment confirmation paper out of his pocket, looked at it and saw that he was supposed to go to the fourth floor. A grumpy looking security guard directed him to the elevators. As soon as Sire walked out of the elevator, he was greeted by another security guard who handed him a number on a piece of paper from which he had pulled out of a machine. "E forty-three," Sire said to himself as he read the number on the piece of paper. He sat next to a lady and her two kids. The large room was crowded, but there were still a lot of available seats. There were monitors displaying ticket numbers and their respective stations all over the room, while a robotic voice called them out. Sire wandered if his number was ever going to get called. "E twenty-two," the robotic voice called out. After waiting for about an hour, Sire's number was finally up on the monitor. He walked up to window number eight and gave his appointment confirmation and identification to the gentleman at the window. He was a white American man with a bald head and a grey mustache. "Let me give you my passport also," Sire said. He went in his back pocket, pulled out his passport and handed it to the agent.

"Where were you born young man?" the agent asked.

"I'm Nigerian."

"How did you end up in Israel?"

"I came with my family. My father is a diplomat."

"Diplomat? I see. Why do you want to go to America?"

Sire froze for a second and scratched his head. A nervous feeling rattled his stomach, like when the teacher asks a question from the homework that was given the previous day, but instead of doing your homework, you were outside hanging with the guys from down the street. *How could he have not been prepared for the most basic question*, he thought. "I want to visit New York, he uttered."

"New York huh, what's over there?" The agent itched his face as if he had just shaven.

*Damn it. Another trivial question*, Sire thought. "I watched Coming to America," he said, "and I would love to see New York in person." Sire was sure that his visa would get denied. How could he have been so unprepared.

"Ah, I like that movie. They should definitely make a sequel."

Sire grinned nervously. "I've watched it like five times," he said.

"Your visa is approved sir," the agent said, "take your passport and this paper and go to the third floor. The agent handed Sire a yellow paper and sent him downstairs.

When Sire returned home that afternoon, Ekema was folding clothes in the living room while the rest of his siblings were still at school. Solomon was at work, and so was his older brother Shelo, who had recently gotten a full-time job at a pharmaceutical plant. "Good afternoon mother," he said, "I was approved."

"Approved? Approved for what my son?"

"My Visa mother, I can travel to New York now."

"What? When did you go to the embassy?"

"I just came back from there a while ago. I had a dream that I was boarding an American Airlines flight, so I booked an appointment."

Ekema was a bit taken aback by the news. Although they had discussed it before, she did not really believe that Sire was going to get his visa. She did not imagine that her son would venture out in the world on his own at nineteen. However, she understood that it was his time to experience life as a responsible adult and become a man. "You have my blessing son," she said, "you must tell your father when he gets home."

Solomon arrived home at his regular time. Standing over six feet tall, he had a towering presence in the house. In African culture, the man of the house was often revered. Solomon's home was no different. He was not extremely strict, but he believed in obedience and taught his children to respect their elders. From a young age, the children, particularly Sire, knew that when Solomon came home, everyone had to be on their best behavior. Even at nineteen, Sire felt fearful whenever he did something that was against his upbringings. He knew his father's thoughts on America, but he had already made his mind up. He waited until Solomon had retired to his bedroom to approach him.

"Good evening father, I would like to discuss something with you," he said.

"Hello son, what is on your mind."

"I went to the American embassy today and I was approved for a visa."

"What? Why did you go to get an American visa?"

Solomon placed the book he was reading on the nightstand next to the bed, while Sire sat on a wooden chair that was near the bedroom door. Ekema had remained in the living room because she wanted to give them some privacy to talk.

"Father I think it's time that I went on my own. I want to go to New York."

"New York? What's over there for you son, you do not know anybody there."

"I have always wanted to go there, since I was a kid."

"I forbid it, you will starve there." Solomon folded his arms and straightened his posture.

"I have already made up my mind."

"I won't allow it, you may be nineteen, but I'm still your father and I say no."

Solomon and Sire reasoned back and forth for a while longer, but neither of them wanted to adhere to the other's point of view. An argument soon ensued, and Sire got so angry that he picked up the wooden chair near the door to throw it at his father, but quickly dropped it when he saw the disappointed look on his father's face. Sire had never disrespected his father in the past but witnessing his father's expression was worse than any punishment. Sire went into his room and laid on his back while watching the ceiling. That night, he did not sleep. He waited until it was five in the morning and went straight to his parent's room to apologize to his father. Sire entered the room and dropped to his knees, begging his father for forgiveness. Ekema had gone to the kitchen to prepare the kids' lunch.

"Stand up son," Solomon said. "America is not an easy place for a black man without working papers." Sire stood up to his feet. "I just want the best for you son, but I have realized that I have to let you learn some things on your own, for you to become a man. You have my blessing Son." Sire reached out and hugged his father. Later that day, he booked a one-way flight to New York for the following week.

## CHAPTER 3

The morning sunlight peered into Sire's room through an opening in the curtain. That was usually enough to awake him. He looked over his shoulder to the other side of the bed, kind of expecting to see Deborah there. He remembered waking up in the middle of the night and feeling her there. Glimpses of her on top of him the night before began playing in his head. He stayed in bed until midday, which was the time that Deborah usually began getting ready for work. After a quick shower, he went downstairs as usual. Deborah was in the kitchen sorting out Edward's lunch. She was wearing an old dress which she had turned into a nightie. Sire remembered seeing her with it when he had woken up in the middle of the night. He waited to see if she would address the elephant in the room. "I left you some food on the stove," she said, giving no indication that she was cognizant of their sexual encounter. Sire followed suit and carried on as he normally would. After Deborah left for work, Sire took Edward to the park to ride his bike. On his way there, Sire looked at Edward walking beside him and thought about Marlon. At only six years old, he looked like a mini version of his father. Without warning, a guilty feeling crept up on Sire. Nevertheless, Marlon's absence made it easier for him to cope. It had been three days since Marlon last visited the house. It also appeared to Sire that Marlon no longer had any affection left for Deborah.

The park was rather crowded on that day. The summer heat had driven the neighboring residents out of their apartments. There were two football teams practicing simultaneously. Others were either exercising or just hanging out in the sun; happy to be out of their stuffy homes. Sire let Edward ride his bike around the track for a little while. He was confident that the beaming sun would wear Edward out in no time. After Edward's fourth spin, the two of them headed back to the house. Edward went upstairs to take a shower, while Sire went to the basement to play some music. He found it difficult to keep his mind off Deborah. Sire was not particularly fond of the tall St. Lucian woman, rather, he saw her as a pleasant distraction from his mundane schedule. Before that night, Sire had never looked at Deborah with lust, nor was he starved for sex. In fact, he was sleeping with two other women in the area at the time.

One of them, Lucille, was staying down the street from Miss Ingrid's house. Sire met Lucille at a hair salon in the area when he first began growing dreads. She had been working there for almost a year, but always complained about the pay. For every customer she serviced, half the money went to the boss. The day Sire walked in, he recognized Lucille's face from the area and decided to sit in her chair. Lucille recognized him as well. When she finished his hair, she slipped Sire her number and told him to call her the next time he needed his hair done. She explained that he could come to her home instead of the shop. That way she could keep the entire profit. Lucille was a curvy, brown skinned girl from Trinidad with thick, straight hair. She was a little older than Sire, who was 21 at the time. One day, Sire went to Lucille's place to get his hair done and they began talking about relationships. The conversation soon turned erotic, and Sire boastfully spoke about being known for "putting in work in the bedroom." After finishing Sire's hair, Lucile stripped down to her underwear, challenging him to uphold his previous statements. Sire took the bait. From that day on, they would meet sporadically when they wanted a release.

The other woman Sire was sleeping with was Heather; a 46-year-old single mom of four. They first met near one of the corner stores in the neighborhood. Sire was walking out the store when she walked past him to go in. He did a double take after noticing Heather's round behind. "You lost something?" she asked. Sire smirked; he loved when women spoke to him in this way. He took it as a challenge. "You can't lose what you never had," he replied. "And if I had you, I'd make sure that I never lose you." Heather was amused by Sire's response. She had an attractive figure and was usually approached by men who made it their duty to point out her huge "ass." Although she could tell that she was much older than Sire, she gave him her phone number. *What harm could it do*, she thought. They soon began flirting via text messages, until one day Sire was invited over to her house. She told him about being married to a drug dealer in the past. She explained that he was the father of her last two children and that he had been deported back to Dominican Republic due to drug trafficking. Before his deportation however, he had put away a large sum of money for Heather and the kids. Sire and Heather grew closer as time went by. Although she had begun to develop feelings for him, Heather understood that Sire was still young. He had a lot of exploring to do before he would be ready to settle down. Sire's companionship, daily text messages, and the occasional visit once or twice a week was adequate. In return, Heather took care of most of Sire's financial needs until he was able to find himself a job.

Sire glanced at the clock; Deborah would be home soon. He had spent half of the day reminiscing on the previous night, and he wanted more. He reasoned that his lust for her stemmed from his fragile state of mind since losing his job. Sire made his way down to the basement and poured himself a drink. It had become part of his daily routine, like washing his face in the morning. By the time Deborah arrived, Edward was almost ready for bed. She usually caught him in the living room watching his cartoons. Other nights, he would fall asleep on the couch if she were running late. Sire listened to Deborah's footsteps while he played Soca music in the basement. He felt a sudden urge to approach her and tell her that she had been on his mind all day. He even thought to tell her that he wanted to have sex again and that it would just be their "dirty little secret." He glanced down, noticed the half-drunk liquor bottle, and realized it was the liquor clouding his mind. He decided to call it a night instead. However, Sire still left his door slightly ajar, just in case Deborah decided to visit. Trying hard not to fall asleep, he began looking at YouTube videos on his phone. Before long, his door squeaked open. But it was not Deborah, it was the wind. Eventually, Sire fell asleep, and he began to dream about Deborah's naked body. In the dream, he felt his pants slide down his legs. He opened his eyes to see that Deborah had returned. This time he took it slow; he wanted it to last.

When Sire awoke that morning, he instinctively looked over his shoulder to the other side of the bed. Deborah was long gone. This time however, he decided that they needed to speak about what had occurred. He went to the kitchen around midday, as normal. Deborah was washing dishes. "Good morning Deborah," he said. "I believe we have something to discuss." Deborah turned around, looked at him briefly and returned her attention to the sink.

"What is there to talk about?" she asked.

"Hmmm…. I don't know, maybe we can start with the weather," he said sarcastically.

"Sure, it's been very wet these last few days," she responded.

"Look, I just want to know what this is, because it seems like some type of spur of the moment thing," stated Sire. Deborah closed the faucet and turned to face him. She was wearing a loose-fitting nightie which showed the imprint of her nipples.

"I've wanted this from the first day I saw you," she said. "I have been secretly in love with you all this time. Wasn't it obvious?"

Sire was taken aback by Deborah's confession. He wondered if Marlon had known about Deborah's secret all this time. He remembered an instance one afternoon, when he was visited by a female friend. Deborah answered the door and told the young lady that Sire was not home, despite seeing him in the kitchen only moments earlier. Sire did not think much of it at the time, but now he viewed it in a different light. Still, he could not have guessed that his best friend's woman was secretly carrying feelings for him. The two of them hardly spoke unless it was about food or Edward.

"I would never have guessed," he said.

"Well, it's the truth. I could not keep my feelings bottled up any longer. I'm sorry for putting you in this predicament. I know how close you and Marlon are but honestly, I'm at a point where I don't care if he finds out. Look at the way he treats me. He doesn't want me and yet can't stand to see me with someone else. He's selfish. I'm sure he's over there cuddled up with his Jamaican girl as we speak."

"That's not true Deborah. The man cares about you. He's just not in the right state of mind right now. And what do you mean you don't care if he finds out? I'm just as guilty as you. Please don't tell that man anything that would lead him to kill the both of us. We should stop before we end up getting caught."

"Don't try to fool yourself. I saw the way you looked at me while I was on top of you. If it wasn't for Edward, I would have moved on a long time ago. I just don't know if I could make it on my own. Things are hard as they are now."

"Look, the sex was great, but I don't want to come between you and Marlon. The man put a roof over my head for God's sake." Deborah interrupted Sire with a kiss while he was speaking.

"I'm going to get ready for work," she said. "We will talk about this later."

Despite his reservations regarding the situation, Sire continued to entertain Deborah's advances. With Marlon and Ingrid gone most of the time, Sire and Deborah indulged in each other with little boundaries. Sire knew that he was playing a dangerous game, but that only made the sex more enjoyable. As time went by, Marlon's relationship with Deborah worsened. Despite openly flaunting his new girlfriend, Marlon still continued to spy on Deborah. He was convinced that she was sleeping with one of her coworkers, so he decided to stalk her after work one night. Marlon borrowed his friend's car and parked across the street from the Home Depot on Utica Avenue, waiting for Deborah to exit. Minutes later, he saw her, and a male coworker leave the store. She got into the man's car, and they drove off with Marlon trailing behind them. However, he got stuck at a red light on Empire Boulevard and lost sight of the car. He gave up the chase and decided to head home, but Deborah did not arrive until an hour later. That night, Marlon and Deborah had a huge fight. He wanted her out of his mother's house immediately. He packed up her belongings in large garbage bags and told her to go back to her aunt.

The next morning, Deborah took all her stuff and moved down the street to Lucille's apartment. The two of them had been friends for years, even before Sire had moved in. Deborah was privy to the fact that Sire and Lucille had been sleeping with each other occasionally. Lucille used to brag about it to her all the time, not knowing that Deborah wanted Sire to herself all along. The more stories she heard, the more curious she became. Lucille had an extra room in her apartment, so she told Deborah that she could stay there until she found a place of her own. Sire did not mind the idea of having two women under the same roof, but he knew that they had to be careful so that Lucille would not suspect anything. There was bound to be some controversy. Lucille was very territorial, despite knowing that she was not the only one that Sire was sleeping with. Sire continued to sleep with Deborah at the house, using Edward as his alibi since he continued to watch him. One night, he fell asleep, and Lucille caught the two of them in bed the next morning. Lucille had gotten up early to use the restroom and found it odd to see Edward sleeping on the living room couch. She peeked into Deborah's room and found her tangled up with Sire under the sheets.

Deborah was right back where she started. After Lucille caught her in bed with Sire, she was told that she could not stay there any longer. Luckily, Deborah had a great relationship with Miss Ingrid, who allowed her to move back into the house in a room upstairs. Around that time, Marlon was having problems with his new girlfriend, so he began spending more time at the house. That did not stop the fun for Sire and Deborah, however, and it did not take long for Marlon to become suspicious of the two. There were two things that triggered his suspicion. For one, whenever Deborah was sharing food, she would make a plate for Sire and leave Marlon to make his own plate. Secondly, Marlon noticed that whenever Sire came around, Deborah's mood would brighten up, regardless of how upset she was. Marlon was eager to get to the bottom of it. One day, while leaving the house, he noticed Lucille walking across the street. He was aware that there had been some type of falling out between Lucile and Deborah, so he decided to try his luck. Marlon asked Lucille if she had noticed anything "funny" going on between Deborah and Sire. Lucille gave Marlon a slight smile, like she was about to solve all his life's problems with some precious piece of intelligence. She told him what she saw when she opened Deborah's door that morning. Her description was very precise, not sparing any details. She even added that they left "poor Eddie" to sleep on the couch. Marlon was angered by this news but maintained his composure until he got back to the house to confront Sire.

Sire was in the basement when Marlon came looking for him. He could tell that something was wrong by the look on Marlon's face. Marlon sat on the couch next to Sire and poured himself a shot of whiskey.

"I feel like we haven't had a good chat in ages," he said.

"I can relate. I've been in my own little world since we lost our jobs."

"Yeah, I know. You know who I just met outside?"

"Who?"

"Lucille. She had a lot to say. She told me some stuff and I just wanted to know if it was true." Marlon turned to face Sire.

"You know Marlon, before I say anything. I think you and Deborah need to have a talk first."

That one line was enough to confirm his betrayal. Marlon was livid, but more than anything, he was hurt. He told Sire that he had until the end of the week to leave, or he would get his cousin Jamal to shoot him. Sire knew Jamal very well. He knew that if Marlon called Jamal, he was as good as dead. Luckily, Heather had already found him a room in East New York. Prior to that day, Sire had begun to feel some tension between him and Marlon. He noticed Deborah's antics when Marlon was around and knew they would get caught sooner or later. He asked Heather to help him find a place to stay and she agreed to pay his rent until he found a job. For the remainder of his stay at Miss Ingrid's, Sire kept as far away from Deborah as possible. He certainly did not want any bullets from Jamal. Moreover, he was almost certain that Marlon had already confronted Deborah about the situation, so he did not feel the need to explain himself.

Before moving to East New York, Sire had only heard the term "crackhead" a few times in his life. Around the time that he moved, the early 2000's, East New York was like a haven for drug addicts and prostitutes. The population there was predominantly minority groups, most of them living in housing developments and project buildings. It wasn't all bad, however. There were lots of hard-working individuals there as well. Some minority families were able to purchase property which they would rent out as an extra source of income. Many of them found it more profitable to divide apartments into smaller rooms. The property where Sire stayed was owned by a Grenadian man who worked as a contractor. It was a two-story apartment building with eight bedrooms, two bathrooms and two kitchens. There were four bedrooms on each floor. Sire's room was on the first floor towards the back of the apartment. He spent most of his time there listening to music. Heather made sure that Sire was fed, and his bills were paid, so he was quite comfortable despite his circumstances.

Nearly two weeks after moving to East New York, Sire received a call from Deborah asking if she could meet with him to speak. Since leaving Brownsville, Sire had not seen nor heard from her. She asked if she could stop by his place after work one night, and he reluctantly agreed. Sire had no idea what Deborah's motives were, but he thought it would have been a good opportunity to get some closure on the situation. That night, Deborah arrived at Sire's place a little after ten in the evening. She was wearing black slacks with a Home Depot t-shirt and was carrying a small Ralph Lauren duffle bag. Sire thought she looked more mature in her work uniform. Immediately after entering the barely furnished room, she broke down in tears. Sire immediately regretted his decision to allow her to come over. Nevertheless, he tried his best to calm her down. She was an emotional wreck. Sire apologized for his role in the affair. He stated that he should have never let it happen in the first place. When Deborah finally stopped crying, Sire thought that her tear glands must have dried up. They spent a short while speaking, and then Deborah stripped down to her underwear before falling asleep on the bed. Sire admired her body while she slept, but then remembered Marlon's threats. He turned his back and smoked a cigarette before falling asleep himself.

The following morning, desire would conquer fear. Sire woke up with an erection and could not summon the strength to resist the enticing St. Lucian woman lying next to him. *Why were men so easily beguiled by the allure of female genitalia*, he wondered. One thing Sire liked about morning sex was that after it was all over, he could start his day off with an open mind, not weighted down by loose sexual cravings. The effects usually faded by midday. Deborah decided not to go to work and instead spent the day laying in bed with Sire. At one point, Sire jumped out of bed and told Deborah to get dressed, like he was awakened from a trance. "You should not be here," he said, "You have a kid to look after." He grabbed her stuff and proceeded to head to the door while her eyes filled with tears. When Sire opened the front door, he noticed someone sitting at the top of the stoop. It was a light-skinned girl with brown eyes. She looked on as he escorted Deborah down the stoop. Deborah kept her head straight while she tried to regain her composure. Sire had to squint as he looked down the block for passing cabs. The sun beamed down on them with great vigor. The girl on the stoop sat comfortably in a shady spot. Soon after, a black gypsy cab cruised down the block. The squeaky brakes sent shivers up Sire's spine as it slowed down. Deborah entered the cab and looked back at Sire as it drove off.

# CHAPTER 4

As soon as Deborah's cab turned the corner, Sire reached into his pocket and grabbed a cigarette. The girl on the stoop asked him if she could get a "buss down," which meant the bottom part of the cigarette. Instead, he reached into his pocket and gave her a whole cigarette. There was an unspoken code among smokers, a sort of mutual understanding. The smoker who carried the pack was expected to share if he or she were asked, knowing one day that they themselves might be in the asking position.

"Need a light?" he asked, while reaching for his lighter.

"Sure," she answered, "I'm Denise by the way. What's your name?"

"Sire."

"Sire? Like a king?"

"Something like that." There was a black gypsy cab coming down the block which resembled the one that Deborah had gotten into. Sire peeked through the window to see if it was her. Somehow, turning the driver around did not seem too farfetched for Deborah to do at the time. Luckily, the cab was empty. Denise realized why he was looking in the cab.

"That was your girlfriend just now?" she asked.

"No, only a friend."

"That's what they all say. Thanks for the cigarette Sire."

A moment later, one of Sire's roommates who lived down the corridor exited the building with her boyfriend. Her name was Rita. "Ready?" she asked Denise, and then the two of them walked down the block. Sire looked on as they left. He was intrigued by Denise's boldness.

The following week on Saturday, one of the tenants in the building was having a birthday party in the backyard. The owner usually allowed tenants to use the backyard for events, as long as they gave him notice ahead of time. This particular tenant was renting one of the rooms on the second floor. Everyone knew him as Greg. He was a short, paunchy man from Barbados. He met Sire in front the building one afternoon and invited him to the party. Sire mentioned that he was a DJ and offered to play for free, as a kind gesture. Greg was quite pleased with the offer and told Sire that he could invite his friends and family. Sire only had one friend at the time. His name was Richie, another one of Marlon's cousins. Like Marlon, Richie was also an experienced DJ. The feud between Sire and Marlon mattered very little to him. He had taken a liking to Sire and probably would have done the same thing in Sire's position. Sire told him to get his equipment ready for the party on Saturday. On the day of the party, Sire introduced Richie to Greg, who requested that they play some old school music for the grown folks. The majority of the people at the party were forty and over. Sire was surprised to see Denise there but figured that she came with Rita. She wore a blue denim dress with white Nike sneakers. She noticed Sire looking at her from behind the DJ booth and gave him a wave and a smile. At one point she walked over to him while he was playing and told him that she wanted to get high. Sire asked Richie to take over the music for a while, and then brought Denise to his room for them to smoke. He was not an avid cannabis smoker, but he usually kept a small bag around for rainy days. When they got to the room, Sire went into his bottom drawer and pulled out a small bag, while Denise sat on the edge of the bed. "I hope you know how to roll it," he said. Denise nodded. Sire turned on the television and told Denise to make herself comfortable, before heading back to the party. He saw one of the tenants next to the DJ booth chatting with Richie, so he went to the bar and poured himself a drink. By the time the party was finished, Sire had consumed so much alcohol that he forgot that he had left Denise in his room. He was surprised to find her still lying in his bed, scrolling through Facebook on her phone.

"Had fun?" she asked him.

"Yea, did you have fun?"

"It's less fun when you're getting high by yourself."

Denise picked up the remainder of the joint and passed it to Sire. Before long, they were making love on the bedroom floor. They did not stop until the sun began to rise, and neither of them wanted to sleep by then. Instead, they thought it was a good time for them to get to know each other. Denise had recently broken up with her boyfriend of four years. She lived across the street from Sire's place with her Panamanian parents and her younger sister Maggie. At age twenty-four, Denise felt like her life was missing something, especially after her relationship ended. Meeting Sire amid her emotional debacle was merely a distraction, some form of temporary refuge.

Since neither of them had a job, Denise spent a considerable amount of time hanging out at Sire's place. Richie would stop by every now and then, especially when he knew that Maggie would be present. She was a tinge darker than Denise and slightly prettier. She had just turned twenty-one, but she did not have as much freedom as Denise. Their father was quite strict. Richie had developed a fondness for Maggie, but secretly she was more interested in Sire, despite him dating her sister. Eventually, Denise caught on to Maggie's hidden agenda, and stopped her from coming around so often. One night, while watching a movie with Richie and Denise, Sire received a call from a strange number. He answered and was surprised to hear his sister's voice on the other end. She told him that their father, who had been battling heart problems for some time now, had just passed away. Sire was devastated by the unfortunate news. He asked her how their mother was doing and then told his sister he loved her.

It took some time for Sire to get over the pain of his father's death. At one point, he considered going back home to be with his family, even though it would mean that he could not return to the United States. After considering all his options, Sire decided that it was best for him to stay. Despite his circumstances at the time, he still believed that he could become a successful singer in New York. About a month after receiving the news of his father's death, Sire received some good news. Denise missed her period and an early pregnancy test yielded positive results. At first, Sire was not sure how to feel about the news. He was not in love with Denise, but as time went by, he started to believe that the baby was the reincarnation of his father. He relayed this to Denise who told him he was becoming delusional. Nevertheless, Sire promised to make Denise and the baby his number one priority. She could not ask for more than that.

It was a breezy afternoon. Sire was walking back home from the Chinese restaurant with food for himself and Denise when he received a call from Richie. There was a massive event taking place in Virginia that weekend, and one of the promoters had asked Richie to play at one of their parties. At the time, Sire had only been as far as New Jersey, so he was delighted when Richie asked him to join him for the weekend trip. They left New York that Friday night and arrived in Virginia early Saturday morning. The drive was a little under six hours. Denise stayed back at the apartment. The day after Sire returned from Virginia, he was approached by Rita in the hallway of the building as he headed out the door. Denise had been spending most of her time with her recently. Rita was a mysterious and petite brunette with tattoos all over her body. She was one of the few Caucasians of whom Sire had seen in East New York. She sometimes wore a bandana around her head and pants that were either very tight or very baggie, like a mixture between hippie and gothic. Around that time, there were rumors going around that Rita was a prostitute, and that her boyfriend was really her pimp. Sire had caught wind of the rumors, but never paid attention to them. He did, however, occasionally notice some odd behavior involving Rita and Denise. At times, they would leave for the entire day and return late in the evening with money and drugs. Still, Sire could not imagine any of them selling their bodies for money. He just thought that they were exceptional con artists. Denise was known for being witty. It was one of things that Sire admired about her.

Rita told Sire that while he was away, she saw Denise bringing multiple guys into his room on different occasions. Sire seemed unbothered by the news. The fact that Rita was speaking to him was more shocking than the news itself. It became apparent that there had been a fall-out between the two girls and Sire wanted no part of it. Rita also told Sire that he should not trust Denise and that she had caught Denise flirting with her boyfriend over the phone. Still, Sire displayed a lack of concern regarding the accusations. He told Rita that whatever feud was going on between herself and Denise had to be sorted out between the two of them. Sire knew that Denise had a lot of male friends, but he did not believe that she would be bold enough to invite any of them to his room.

A few days later, a relative of Denise advised her to apply for government assistance to pay for groceries. She asked Sire to accompany her to the WIC office in Downtown Brooklyn to fill out an application. Sire dreaded waking up early in the morning, but Denise wanted to beat the crowd. They took the train from

New Lotts Avenue and arrived Downtown just after 9:00am. Denise was slightly annoyed with Sire because she struggled to wake him up on time. He kept asking for five more minutes. By the time he finally woke up, Denise was fully dressed and had a full-blown attitude. Sire had grown accustomed to Denise's occasional moodiness. He was more concerned with getting back home in time to catch some more sleep before the morning was over.

The line at the WIC office was long, and it wrapped around the service area like a snake. There was a female security guard standing near the entrance. She was a chubby Hispanic woman with a grim look on her face. Sire pitied her. He could not imagine having to deal with moody, pregnant women all day. She directed them to the back of the line and then clicked the hand-held tally counter she was holding twice. There were four customer service agents working at the time and by the way they were moving, Sire knew they would be standing in line way past lunch time. He looked down at Denise's stomach and felt bad that she had to stand in the endless line. She had a doctor's appointment the day before, but Sire did not go because he overslept. He did not feel guilty about it until then.

"How was the doctor's visit yesterday?" he asked.

"It went well."

"Next time I won't oversleep."

"Next time I'll pour water on your head."

Sire smiled, knowing that she would really do it. He admired that side of Denise: the bold and crazy side. The line was moving faster than Sire had anticipated. Most of the people in line were women under the age of thirty. The few men that were there were just accompanying their girlfriends or wives. Sire noticed a sign hanging above the customer service booth. "Women, Infants and Children Center," it read. That's when he realized what WIC actually meant.

"So how far along are you?" he asked.

"The doctor said four months."

"Okay, so the baby is due in May."

"Yes, our due date is May 21st."

By the time they left the WIC office, Sire had a strong craving for a cigarette and a cup of coffee. They stopped by a Deli on Fulton Street before heading to the train. The ride back to East New York was a lot more crowded, but Sire was able to find a seat for Denise. He stood directly in front of her, staring down at her slightly bulging stomach. He realized how much her pregnancy had begun to change her body. *When you see someone every day, you do not notice how much they change right before your eyes*, he thought. Suddenly, his mind wandered back to their earlier conversation at the WIC office. Denise had mentioned that she was four months pregnant, but it had been less than three months since she and Sire met. For the remainder of the ride home Sire tried to make sense of this in his head, but it just wasn't adding up.

As they exited the train, Denise couldn't help but notice that Sire's demeanor had changed. The look on his face resembled the one he had when he learned of his father's death.

"What's wrong?" she asked.

"Are you sure you're four months pregnant?"

"Well according to the doctor, yes. What's the problem?"

"The problem, is that we met three months ago."

Denise stopped in the middle of the sidewalk and turned to look at Sire.

"Well maybe the doc made a mistake," she said.

"A mistake?"

"Yes, it happens. You think this is not your child?"

Sire recalled that when he met Denise, she had just broken up with her boyfriend. Then, he thought about what Rita had told him about Denise, along with the prostitution rumors. By the time they arrived at the apartment, Sire was convinced that he was not the father of that baby. As soon as they walked in, an argument ensued regarding the matter. Denise was adamant that the baby was Sire's, but his mind was made up. He told Denise that he needed some time to think, so she packed up all her belongings and moved back across the street with her parents.

After just two days apart, Sire missed Denise immensely. He grappled with the possibility that the baby could actually be his, and that the doctor could have simply made a mistake. He could not help feeling guilty for abandoning her. One afternoon, he decided that he was going to get her back. He went to the flower shop and bought the most luxurious looking bouquet of flowers he could find. After purchasing the flowers, he went back home to tidy up just in case he was able to get her to come home with him. That afternoon, the weather was extremely hot, but Sire chose to wear his favorite long-sleeve shirt. As he walked out the door, he realized that he had forgotten the bouquet on his dresser, so he went back inside to retrieve it. The plan was simple, he thought. He was going to ring her doorbell and present her with the flowers and a heart-felt apology. After one more look in the mirror, he headed out the door. As he was crossing the street however, he noticed two people exiting Denise's house. He stood next to a tree and waited until they were closer to the street to get a better view. Once he saw who It was, he turned around and headed back to his apartment. It was Denise, strolling out the house with her ex-boyfriend. Sire could tell it was him because he had seen pictures of the two of them on Denise's Facebook page. A tall light-skinned man, probably in his late twenties. They seemed happy as they walked towards his car. Denise was all smiles. When he got back inside, Sire put the bouquet back on the dresser, and picked up the bottle of Hennessey that was on the floor next to his bed.

After seeing Denise together with her ex, Sire decided that he was going to leave her alone for good. He even began to consider moving out of the area. He had grown increasingly fed up with seeing all the junkies on his block every time he left the apartment. The final straw came when he stepped on a used needle that nearly punctured his slippers. After returning to his apartment, Sire called Heather and told her to help him find another room. Heather made a few phone calls and was able to find him a vacant room in a Brownsville apartment building. He moved out the following week without saying a word to anyone in the building, except the landlord. Sire did not mind being back in Brownsville. He was just glad to be away from the drug activity. However, Brownsville was not much better, it was just less obvious.

**CHAPTER 5**

One morning, Sire woke up to a few missed calls. A quick check revealed that they were all from Maggie, Denise's sister. Sire had exchanged numbers with her before leaving East New York. He had planned on hooking her up with Richie but realized that she was more interested in him. He got out of bed, lit a cigarette, and returned her call. "Hey Maggie," he said. "Is everything okay?" She told him that she was going through some tough times and needed someone to talk to. Sire was delighted at the idea of being a therapist for a day. It was not like he had anything better to do. He sent her his new address and she arrived there within the hour. Sire was surprised at how fast she came. He was just about to hop in the shower. She was wearing long grey tights and a black top. Her skin tone was a bit darker than her sister's, but their body types were quite similar. Sire told her that she could sit on the bed while he went to take a shower. By the time he was done, Maggie had fallen asleep. She slept for hours, while Sire tried his best not to wake her. He felt like every move he made sounded ten times louder than normal. When she finally woke up, Sire was on his laptop looking for instrumentals on YouTube. She apologized for taking up his bed and space; his room was not the most spacious one. They started talking and she told him that Denise had given birth to a baby girl, and that her boyfriend had moved into the apartment with them. She said that Denise was insecure and didn't trust her around her boyfriend. Sire took his focus off Maggie for a second, as if he were staring into blankness. "Do you have any pictures of the baby?" he asked. Maggie told him that she had recently gotten a new phone and had not transferred all her pictures over yet.

"So, what did you want to talk about?" Sire asked.

"I've been a bit stressed lately. I haven't been sleeping enough."

"Well, it can't be insomnia. I watched you sleep for hours."

Maggie smiled, embarrassed. "Ever since Denise's baby father moved in, I haven't been able to get any privacy. The baby cries a lot at night and on top of that, the two of them argue like crazy."

"I see."

"To make matters worse, I think he has a crush on me, and Denise notices the way he looks at me sometimes. It makes me extremely uncomfortable."

Sire knew that there had been tension between the two sisters in the past. He thought it was normal for sisters around the same age to compete for the same man. "She's just a bit jealous," he said. "It's quite normal."

"Hmmmm." Maggie looked away.

"Don't you have a boyfriend?"

"Not anymore. We broke up a few months ago."

"Remember Richie, my friend?" He asked. "He had told me that he has a crush on you."

"Yea I remember him. But he's not my type."

"Okay, that's cool. Well, I'm not dating anyone right now, so feel free to come over whenever you need to escape."

Maggie smiled. "I have work this afternoon, so I'm going home to get ready. Thanks for speaking with me Sire."

"I should open a therapy office," he replied jokingly.

For the next few weeks, Maggie would visit Sire sporadically, when she needed to "escape." Sometimes she would spend only a few hours and other times the entire day. Eventually, the two of them became intimate. One day, while Sire was hanging out with Richie, she popped up unexpectedly. Sire tried to convince her to have a threesome with the two of them, but she declined. Her feelings for Sire were growing and she did not want him to view her in a bad light. Sire was chary where Maggie was concerned. After what happened with Denise, he did not want to fall for another woman so soon.

As time went by, Sire grew tired of not working and having to depend on Heather for money all the time. One Friday, Richie got invited to an event, so he brought Sire along with him. It had been a while since the two of them went out. When they arrived there, they met up with an old friend of Richie named Milo. They had met at a DJ clash some years prior. Richie introduced him to Sire and the three of them headed over to the bar for drinks. Sire noticed that Richie spoke in two accents. One of them American, and the other Guyanese. He switched back and forth flawlessly, depending on what he was saying or who he was speaking to. Since moving to New York, Sire noticed how easy it was for people to switch back and forth from an American accent to their native tongue, like some type of art. By the end of the night, Sire and Milo had built a good rapport, and exchanged phone numbers.

About a week after meeting Milo, Sire was doing laundry when his phone rang. He did not recognize the number but decided to answer. "Hello?" he said.

"Hello sir. How are you. This is Shawn. I got your number from Milo."

"From who?" For a split second, Sire had forgotten all about meeting Milo at the event.

"Milo. I'm his cousin. He told me that you might be looking for work."

"Oh, Milo. Yes, I did mention that to him."

"I work at a car dealership on Utica Avenue. We are looking for someone to wash the cars. The pay is three hundred dollars per week in cash. Is that something you would be interested in?"

"Yea sure, I'm interested." Sire thought that if someone was willing to pay him three hundred dollars a week to play with water all day, he would be a fool not to take it. "When can I start?"

"Come in tomorrow morning at ten. I'll text you the address now."

The following day, Sire arrived at the dealership a little after nine in the morning. The gates were still locked when he arrived, so he went to the donut shop across the street to buy coffee. Utica Avenue was busier than usual that morning, with dollar-vans holding up traffic as they stopped abruptly to pick up passengers. In one instance, a man driving a Nissan Maxima exited his vehicle to confront one of the dollar van drivers who was blocking him off. Sire sat and watched the theatrics from inside the donut shop, while sipping his coffee and keeping an eye on the time. He had arrived at the dealership quite early, despite spending a lot of time trying to decide what to wear. He wanted to dress business casual in order to make a good first impression. However, his job was to wash the cars in the lot, and he did not want to be overdressed either. He ultimately decided to wear black windbreaker pants and a black t-shirt.

Sire had almost finished his coffee when he looked across the street and saw an Arabian man pulling up the gates to the dealership. He waited until the gates were all the way up, then walked across the street. The man was wearing a turban, but he was also dressed in a suit. Sire assumed that he was the manager or probably one of the owners.

"Good morning sir," He said. "My name is Sire. Shawn asked me to come in today."

"Oh, you're the guy he was telling me about. Okay Shawn will be here in a few minutes, then he will tell you what to do. You can sit in the office while you wait."

"Okay sir, no problem." Sire sat in the chair nearest to the window. Inside, the office was much bigger than it had looked from the outside. There were two desks. Each of them was equipped with a desktop computer, phone, and other office supplies. There was a private room within the office, with a door that had the word "Manager," painted in blue. Sire looked around for a restroom but realized that it was located outside the office in a separate shed. He heard the Arabian man speaking on the phone from within the manager's room. Suddenly, the front door opened. A slender-looking man walked in.

"Good morning. Sire, right?"

"Good morning. Yes, that's me."

"I'm Shawn. Give me a minute. I'll show you where the equipment is."

Shawn laid his stuff down on one of the desks and took Sire outside to a small room towards the back of the lot. "So, you met Yousuf?" he asked.

"You mean the Arab guy. Yea, but he didn't say much."

"Yea, that's definitely Yousuf. He's one of the owners. Mo is a bit kinder. He's the other owner. And then there's Sandra, the finance manager. She's out for a few days."

They arrived at the small equipment room. Inside, there was a long green water hose, two buckets, a few bags of soap, and some used rags piled up in a heap. Sire picked up the hose and got straight to work. He knew what he had to do- make the cars look presentable for potential buyers. He started with the cars in the front and gradually made his way towards the ones in the back.

Shawn was a salesman. Sire watched as he approached potential buyers and studied the way in which he spoke to them. It seemed like a second language, made up of a mixture of half-truths, flattery, and subterfuge. One afternoon, Shawn was helping a customer, when a tall, dark-skinned man wearing a baseball cap and a hoodie asked to check out a grey Ford truck at the front of the lot. Shawn asked Sire to sit in the truck with the man so that he could take it for a test drive around the block. As soon as they turned the corner onto Snyder Avenue, the man pulled out a long, army-styled knife from his pocket and told Sire to get out of the truck. Sire wasted no time. He hopped out of the truck while keeping a close eye on the knife. The man sped down Snyder Avenue towards East 49th Street, before making a right turn, disappearing from Sire's view. Sire was still in shock, and it took him a moment to react. He looked around to see if anyone had witnessed the robbery, then dialed 9-1-1. When Shawn saw Sire walking back to the dealership, he knew instantly that something had gone awry. Sire told Shawn what had transpired. It was at that exact moment Shawn realized that he had forgotten to make a copy of the man's driver's license before letting him take the car for a test drive. Facing Yousuf was going to be the worst part. Shawn knew that he would not let this incident go without some type of penalty.

Business at the dealership had soon returned to normalcy shortly after the robbery. As punishment, Sire and Shawn agreed to give up a percentage of their weekly salary until the balance of the stolen car was fully paid off. Luckily, the car was on sale for only three thousand dollars. As time went by, Sire became increasingly confident that he could master the salesman position. One day, he waited until Mo was alone in the office to inquire about a promotion. "All right," Mo said. "I want you to follow Shawn around for the rest of the week. Study everything that he does. When you come back to work on Monday, you'll be coming in as a salesman." Sire followed Mo's instructions, mirroring

Shawn's every move: the demeanor, smile, and lingo. Shawn had developed a good relationship with Sire since they began working together, so he did not mind showing him the ropes.

Monday finally arrived. Sire was eager to begin his first day as a salesman. It only took him three hours to close his first sale. After only four weeks in his new position, Sire's productivity surpassed that of Shawn. When he saw how much money he was making as a salesman, he became interested in the finance manager position, which paid nearly twice as much. After each sale, Sire would sit down with Sandra, studying the way in which she dealt with the banks. One day, he overheard Shawn saying that Sandra was about to resign. Without wasting time, he went to Mo to inquire about the position. He was pleased to learn that Mo had already considered him for the position and was planning to tell him about a week before Sandra's resignation date. Unfortunately, on the day that he was to begin training, Yousuf brought in his nephew to fill the position instead. It was a major let down for Sire, who was more than ready to take on the new position.

Overtime, the two owners began to disagree on key business decisions. They had been in business together for over twelve years, but a clash of egos caused them to part ways. Eventually, Mo opened his own dealership in Sunnyside Queens. As soon as it was up and running, he called Sire with a proposal. He was willing to offer him a finance manager position if he would leave Yousuf's dealership. Without giving it a second thought, Sire accepted Mo's offer and gave Yousuf his two-week's notice. With Sire's help, Mo was able to turn the dealership into a success in a short period of time. After only seven months in business, he opened a second dealership in Brooklyn. As the business progressed, Sire's workload increased twofold. There was little time for anything else besides working and sleeping. One Sunday, Sire decided to make some time to go visit Heather. They had not spoken for some time, and he was beginning to suffer from sexual starvation. When he arrived at the house, he saw two of Heather's kids playing with a ball in the yard. The moment they saw him, they told him that their mother had gotten a new boyfriend. He found it quite amusing. Afterall, they were just kids. When he entered the house, he saw Heather moping the kitchen floor. She was wearing a yellow summer dress. She had a few strands of grey hair which were barely noticeable. She would dye her hair black every now and again, but Sire preferred when she allowed the grays to grow in naturally. He told Heather what the kids said to him out front. She looked at him and smiled with pity. That's when he knew it was true. Heather put the mop down, they went into the living room to talk. She sat on the couch and patted the space beside her, gesturing Sire to sit.

"I met someone," she said.

"So, it's true. When were you planning on telling me this?"

"Well, you have been missing for some time now. I know you're busy with work and getting your life together. I figured that I was the least of your concerns. Besides, it wasn't something I had planned. It was an old friend who contacted me on Facebook, and he asked me to go out with him. Before I knew it, we were texting each other every day. He's a little older than I am but he seems to be really serious about me."

"I see." Sire scratched his forehead.

"Sire, you have your whole life ahead of you. I'll always love you but I'm not getting any younger."

Sire's conversation with Heather ended on an agreeable note. Although he was slightly hurt, he was glad that Heather had found someone to settle down with. She had a good heart and spirit and deserved to be happy. He wished that he had treated her better instead of just relying on her for sex and financial support. Now that he had a job and could stand on his own two feet, he thought the least he could do was be happy for her. The following day, at the dealership, Sire tried his best to focus on his work, but he was distracted by thoughts of Heather. As he sat there daydreaming, the phone rang. It was Mo. "Hey can you stay in a bit later tonight?"

he asked. "I want to talk to you about something." Sire spent the remainder of the day in suspense, wondering what Mo wanted to discuss with him. When he finished helping his last customer, he sent Mo a text asking him what time he would arrive at the dealership. Mo showed up shortly after with a bottle of Jack Daniels Whiskey. By this time, everyone else had already left. "Let's make a toast," he said. Sire stood up and asked what they were celebrating. Mo was a few inches taller than Sire. He had a bald head and a bushy beard. He was wearing a button-down shirt with the top buttons left open, displaying a large gold necklace. He told Sire that he was pleased with the progress that they had made working together. He offered him a managerial position and salary increase at a new Brooklyn location. They were doing great in Queens, but Mo needed someone he could trust to handle day-to-day operations in Brooklyn. Sire was thrilled with the new proposition. The two men shook hands and enjoyed a few shots of rum.

The following week, Sire walked into his new place of employment with a pair of black skinny jeans and a navy-blue button-down shirt. The first person he noticed was Dave, who was pulling up the front gates. Dave was the salesman at the time; a tall, clean-shaven man from Sri Lanka. After introducing himself, Dave brought him inside the office to meet Eva, the finance manager. "Eva, meet Sire. Your new manager," he said. Sire saw the voluptuous, full-figured woman sitting at her desk with a black t-shirt that read "Don't Try Me." She gave Sire a quick zipper smile and focused her attention back to what she was doing on her computer. The Brooklyn branch was much smaller than the one in Queens, consisting of only three workers. Overtime, Eva eventually warmed up to Sire. One slow afternoon, they were discussing their sex lives and after hearing Sire's stories, Eva asked him to pull his pants down so that she could have a look. Sire quickly obliged, revealing his private parts to Eva without hesitation. "What are you going to do about it?" he asked. Eva simply rolled her eyes and asked Sire to pull his pants back up.

C
H
A
P
T
E
R
6

Winter was quickly approaching. Fallen leaves filled the streets of Brooklyn. Despite having added responsibilities with his new managerial position, Sire still found time to pick up a few party gigs. He formed a DJ group consisting of himself, Richie, and Milo. They called themselves "The Triple Threat." Ironically though, the only threat was between each other. The group soon split up after touring NYC due to Richie and Milo arguing. They were scheduled to play at a popular event in Queens but could not agree on who should play first. Despite Sire's efforts to create peace between the two, their egos got in the way of reason. Subsequently, Richie took his laptop and left the event. Luckily, Sire always carried his laptop with him to every event. After that night, Sire and Milo continued working events together, while Richie kept himself at a distance. Sire had no issues with Richie, however, so they kept in contact with each other occasionally.

With the two of them spending more time around each other, Sire noticed some characteristics of Milo that he was not too fond of. For one, Milo had a narcissistic personality. He always assumed that he was right about everything, and things had to be done his way or no way at all. Despite Milo's issues however, Sire kept him close because they were making a lot of money together. One Saturday, they were playing at a birthday party in Crown Heights, when Sire noticed a familiar face in the crowd. It was none other than Marlon, standing by the bar waiting for a drink. The two of them had not spoken or seen each other since Sire moved out of Miss Ingrid's house. Sire wasn't sure how Marlon would react to seeing him, but nevertheless, he made his way towards the bar. To his surprise, Marlon looked happy to see him. They greeted each other as brother's would and proceeded to have a drink together. Marlon told Sire that shortly after he left, Deborah announced that she was engaged to someone she had met online.

"I don't know how long she knew this guy, honestly," he said. "One day I saw her packing her stuff and before you knew it, she was gone. I told her she wasn't taking my son to live with no stranger, so I'm home with Eddie most of the time."

"Wow, I never heard her mention anything about online dating. By the way, I never formally apologized for what had occurred between me and her, but I'm truly sorry. You looked out for me when I had nothing."

"Don't worry about it. These things happen. You were in a bad mental state, and she took advantage of that. She played the both of us. Anyways buddy, how's life treating you. You find a job yet."

"Yea man. I'm managing a dealership in East Flatbush. Besides that, I've been doing the DJ thing on the weekends to make some extra cash. You know Milo, right?

"You mean Richie's friend. Yea I met him a few times while I was out playing. He's a well-known DJ."

"Yeah, he had a falling out with Richie the other day, over some dumb stuff. He's a bit arrogant but for now we are making good money together."

"Well, I'm glad you're doing good buddy. I have a friend trying to get me into some construction work. I'm tired of being at home."

"Amen to that."

Back at the dealership on Monday morning, Sire and Eva sat in the office discussing their recent weekend activities. Eva had gone Upstate to visit some family members on Saturday. As Sire was telling her about his encounter with Marlon, he was interrupted by a loud honking outside. He looked out the window and saw a familiar-looking car, a red Toyota Camry. He stepped outside to see who it was and noticed the smile on the female driver's face. Her name was Kezzie. Sire had met her a few weeks prior when she came to the dealership to purchase the Camry. He remembered that day quite well. Kezzie walked into the dealership wearing a tight-fitting black dress and a pair of stilettos heels. She saw the red Camry and told Sire to get the car ready for her because she was paying in cash. Sire obliged; he was amused by Kezzie's boldness. Before she left the dealership, Sire asked her for her number. Ever Since that day, Sire and Kezzie began a flirtatious relationship, which soon turned romantic. Kezzie wanted to surprise Sire by bringing him lunch, so she showed up outside the dealership unannounced. For Sire, it was a pleasant surprise.

Later that afternoon, Sire received a call from Milo regarding two upcoming gigs. The first one was scheduled for that coming Saturday, and other was scheduled for the following weekend. Sire had gotten accustomed to sporadic calls from Milo of that nature. Milo was quite popular in the DJ community, partaking in several clashes and playing at large events. Sire enjoyed DJing as a hobby and as an extra source of income, but his true passion was to become a singer. He had begun putting together a home studio, buying new pieces of equipment whenever he got paid. So far, he has gotten a mike, headphones, pro-tools, monitor and speakers. It took some time, but gradually he began to figure out how to manipulate the equipment to get his voice and the instrumentals to sound melodic. He created a YouTube channel after completing a few songs. This would mark the beginning of Sire's singing career.

It was finally Saturday. Sire secured the gates to the dealership and headed home to get ready for the party. On his way home, he stopped at the deli near the dealership to purchase a pack of black and mild cigars. There was an older lady sitting in front of the deli on her walker. She had a clear plastic cup in her hand which contained a couple dollars and some coins. Sire was quite familiar with her from his frequent trips to the deli. He always dropped a few coins in her cup on his way out. That evening, Sire felt particularly generous. After purchasing his cigars, he paid for a sandwich and a drink and told the clerk that it was for the "sweet old lady" sitting outside. On his way out he slipped a ten-dollar bill in her cup, and she uttered "thank you baby," as she always did. By the time he got home, there were two missed calls on his phone. Both were from Richie. He did not want to be unprepared when Milo came to pick him up, so he went in the shower before returning Richie's call. Once he was out the shower, he rang Richie.

"Hey Rich, what's up?" he asked.

"Hey man, what's up. You busy right now?"

"I'm getting ready to head out in a few, but what you need though?"

"I'm playing at a party on Dumont and Saratoga, but I need to make a quick run."

"Okay, so do you need me to hold it down."

"Yeah, only for about half an hour."

"Okay I'll be there in a minute."

Sire got dressed and headed to Richie's party. It was only a five-minute walk from his house. On his way there, he sent a text to Milo with the address, letting him know to pick him up from there instead of his apartment. It was one of those basements that was used for throwing underground parties. As soon as Sire arrived, Richie introduced him to the host and told him that he would return in thirty minutes. Richie's mother had locked her keys in their apartment, and she was stuck outside. The first thing Sire noticed was the number of good-looking women that were there. He kind of wished he did not have to attend Milo's event. Once Richie returned to the party, he stepped out of the basement to call Milo, but there was no answer. A glance at the time revealed that it was almost 11:00pm. Milo's event should have already started by then. Nonetheless, Sire was having a good time at the basement party, so he went back inside in search of a woman to dance with. He met a girl that he knew from the neighborhood. Everyone called her Shay. She was wearing a short blue dress that looked like it was going to rip with the slightest of movements. Her blonde wig almost completely covered her small oval-shaped face. Richie began playing slow Reggae music, so Sire reached out his hand towards her to ask for a dance.

Sire was having such a good time with Shay that he forgot all about Milo's party. He waited until everyone left and began helping Richie pack up his equipment. The next morning, Sire woke up with a slight headache. He reached for a cigarette from the pants that he wore the night before and sat up on the bed. He remembered Shay putting her number in his phone but did not feel the urge to call or text. While scrolling through Facebook, it became obvious that Milo had stood him up. He saw pictures of Milo at the event they were supposed to work together. Still, the following Saturday, they were booked to play at a baby shower. The girl that booked them, Shawna, was someone that they knew mutually. She was hosting the baby shower for her cousin Candace, who was seven months pregnant at the time. Sire called Shawna and told her that something had come up and that he was not going to be available to do the party anymore. He assured her that Milo would be able to do the party on his own. Sire thought it was best for him to stay away from Milo for some time. He placed the cigarette bud on the ash tray near the bed and went back to sleep.

On Monday morning, Sire went to work feeling refreshed. He had slept for most of the day on Sunday, only getting up to eat and smoke. His decision to distance himself from Milo brought him some peace of mind as well. Kezzie had already called him twice for the morning, but he was too busy to call her back. The two of them had recently become intimate, causing Kezzie to become more possessive. Sire wasn't entirely surprised, however. Experience had taught him that women's feelings tended to grow with sex. For him, it was the opposite. After the initial sexual encounter, his enthusiasm and interest would drop. Kezzie had a fiery personality which Sired admired, but she was also quite cantankerous.

Sire tried calling back Kezzie when he got a break from work but reached her voicemail instead. After he did not hear back from her for several hours, he assumed that she was busy. A few days had gone by and there was still no word from Kezzie, even after multiple texts and phone calls from Sire. On Saturday, the day of the baby shower, Sire had some idle time at the dealership, so he decided to visit Kezzie's Facebook page to see if there were any recent posts from her. He quickly regretted that decision after he saw a recent photo of Kezzie kissing another man in front of a restaurant. The picture was posted the previous day. Sire took a long hard look at the picture. Kezzie was wearing a white see-through top with denim shorts. Her hair was up in a ponytail which gave her an innocent appearance. Her eyes were closed shut as her lips were locked with those of a tall, well-built, black man. The two of them looked perfect together. Almost too perfect, like they were posing for a magazine picture. He could not help but feel slightly inadequate, so he blocked her. Throughout the day, Sire tried his best to keep the photo out of his head, but he needed some type of distraction besides work. There was the baby shower that evening, but he would have to settle things with Milo first. After much thought, Sire finally decided to call Milo to set the record straight. They had a brief conversation, and then Milo agreed to pick Sire up at seven o'clock that evening.

Sire had just finished putting on his clothes when he thought he heard a car honking outside. He looked out the window and saw Milo's black Nissan maxima double parked across the street. He sprayed on some cologne and headed down to meet him. It had been quite some time since the two of them hung out together. They arrived at the event space on Beverly Road around 7:30pm. The venue was spacious and filled with pink decorations and ornaments. On a small stage towards the front, there was a large silver chair that looked like it was built for a queen. There was also an elevated DJ booth towards the back of the room. It was hard to believe that it was a baby shower, but Sire knew the host Shawna, and she did everything extravagantly. There was another DJ playing when they entered, but they were scheduled to go on at eight. Sire noticed some familiar faces. He looked around for Shawna and saw her next to the stage speaking with the mother-to-be and another girl who looked like she was mixed with Indian and Black. Sire went to say hello to them while Milo went to the DJ booth to set up the equipment. As soon as Shawna saw Sire, she ran up to him and embraced him with a hug. He had done events for her in the past. She introduced him to Candace, the mother-to-be, and Sandy, her Guyanese friend. Sire took a good long look at Sandy. She was pretty and curvaceous with dark brown skin and dark Indian hair. She had a curious look on her face, like a child looking at a new toy for the first time. Sire gave her a flirtatious smile. He welcomed anything that could distract him from thinking about Kezzie.

The venue became more crowded as time passed. It was around the time when everyone was either drunk or tipsy, and the dance floor was packed to capacity. Sire had been playing for a while, so he let Milo take over and decided to head to the bar to refill his cup. On his way back from the bar, he bumped into

Sandy, who immediately accosted him for a dance. They danced for a short while, and then Sire took Sandy's number before returning to the DJ booth. By the time the party had ended, Sire was fully drunk. Luckily, Milo was still sober, so he packed up the equipment on his own and dropped Sire off at his place. Sire stumbled up the stairs to his room and managed to land on his bed.

The next morning, Sire woke up feeling hung over and horny. He scrolled through his contact list, skipped over a few names, and landed on Sandy's number. He vaguely remembered there being some chemistry between them the previous night, but she did not seem like the type of woman that would sleep with someone that she had just met. However, with Kezzie out of the picture and Maggie's visits becoming few and far in between, he figured it was worth a shot. The phone rang three times, and then Sandy picked up.

"Hello?" she said.

"Hello Sandy, do you know who this is."

"I think so. Is it Sire?"

"No, it's Sire's ghost."

"You're funny." Sandy laughed.

"So they say."

"So, what's up?"

"Not much, I just woke up and you were the first thing on my mind."

"Really? Let me guess, you woke up with a boner and remembered that you got my number last night."

Sire laughed. "Well, the boner part is true. But that wasn't the reason I called," he said.

"Sure, I hear ya."

"So, what do you have planned for the day." He asked.

"Nothing really."

"Wanna come over. I could use some company today."

"Hmmmm, company huh?"

"Yea, you know. Just to chat."

"Okay, text me your address."

There was some level of delight that came with the anticipation of novel sex, like travelling to a new country. Sire quickly jumped in the shower after hanging up with Sandy. While he was getting dressed, he saw his phone vibrate. It was a text from Sandy saying that she was outside. He went to open the door and saw Sandy standing at the bottom of the stoop. She was dressed in a black North Face jacket with black tights. Her hair was worn in similar fashion as the night before: a ponytail with a few strands sticking out like she had been shocked by static. It was a subtle, natural look that Sire was not too familiar with. Most of the women in the neighborhood were usually seen sporting long weaves and long eyelashes. Sandy was simple, but beautiful. Her face lit up with a smile when Sire opened the door. Once upstairs, Sire told her to make herself comfortable. She looked around the room, observing Sire's habitat, and then sat on the computer chair. She noticed the mike stand next to the computer. "So, you're a DJ and a singer?" She asked. Sire blushed and said that he was a jack of all trades. Sandy took off her top. "I'll be the judge of that," she said.

The sex was intense, leaving them both drenched in sweat when it was over. For what seemed like a moment, but was probably hours, they laid in bed staring up at the ceiling. Time was non-existent. There was only sweat and oxygen. Now that the sex was out of the way, it was time for the two of them to get to know each other. Sire was open and eager. It marked a pivotal point in his love life. For the first time in his life, he really wanted to know someone beyond the physical. At twenty-two, Sandy was a few years younger than Sire, but she spoke with a high level of maturity. She had spent half of her life in her native country Guyana, and then migrated to New York with her parents when she was a teenager. Sire listened attentively to stories of Sandy's childhood. He ordered food for the both of them, and by the time they were finished eating the sun was beginning to set. Shortly after, Sandy begun getting dressed to leave. She bent over to put on her tights in a teasing fashion. Sire had a weakness for that kind of role-play and could not resist an invitation for a second round.

The weather was rather warm for October. Sire was walking back to the dealership from the Deli down the street. He opted for a red bull energy drink instead of the usual coffee. It had been just over a week since him and Sandy met, and things were going good between the two of them. Although they had not seen each other since the day she came to visit him, they spoke on the phone often. As he was approaching the dealership, Sire noticed a familiar-looking car parked near the front. He could not believe it. Just when he was moving on with his life, here comes Kezzie to terrorize him, he thought. As soon as she noticed him walking towards the entrance of the lot, she flicked her headlights on and off, signaling him to come to the car. For a second, Sire thought about ignoring her completely. However, Kezzie was always up for a challenge. She would have sat outside the dealership all day until he came back out. He walked over to her car and sat in the passenger seat.

"Miss me yet?" She asked.

"How can I miss something I never had?"

"What's that supposed to mean?"

"Why are you here Kezzie?"

"I wanted to see you."

"I'm sure you have lots of other people to see. I gotta get back to work."

Kezzie put her hand near Sire's crotch. "Can I come over tonight?" She asked.

Sire took a good look at Kezzie and wondered what he saw in her. She was wearing a white cap, probably because her hair was not done. She did not have her usual glow, but even then, he found it difficult to avoid getting beguiled by her sexual prowess. "I'll be home by seven," he said.

On his way home from work that evening, Sire stopped at the liquor store to purchase a bottle of E&J Brandy, a deviation from the usual Hennessey bottle. After showering, he had a few shots while he anticipated Kezzie's arrival. He was nearly drunk by the time she arrived. She was wearing a long black coat that passed her knees. As soon as she entered Sire's room, she took the coat off, revealing nothing but her underwear underneath it. She then sat on Sire's lap and leant over for a kiss. Sire indulged in Kezzie's body, like an entrée. As soon as it was over, a feeling of guilt crept up on him like a thief in the shadows. Sandy was on his mind then. He knew that she had begun to fall for him, but he also knew that he was not ready to settle down with one woman. After Kezzie left, Sire sent Sandy a text message telling her that he was not right for her and that she needed to head for the hills. He fell asleep shortly after with the bottle of Brandy next to him. The next morning, Sire woke up to a text message from Sandy telling him that she was going to leave him alone. It left him feeling unsettled, but at the time he thought it was the best thing for the both of them. He did not want to draw her in, only to hurt her in the end. Kezzie was by no means loyal to him, but she made time to see him every now and again, and that was enough for him. At that time, all Sire wanted to do was flirt, have fun, and make music. He had acquired just about everything that was needed for a standard home studio. With his singing improving gradually, he gained an appreciation for his music and his solitude.

A few weeks had gone by since Sire and Sandy had last spoken. He found himself daydreaming about her a lot in recent days. One evening, he was at home browsing through social media, when he noticed a picture of her on Shawna's Facebook page. She was wearing a white dress with a straw hat. She looked slightly younger in that picture. Sire remembered the intense sex they had together. It was at that moment he realized that he had made a mistake. He felt determined to get Sandy back one way or the other. After some thought, he sent her a long text message explaining why he had suddenly abandoned her, adding that he did not intend to cause her grief. Sandy did not respond to Sire's text until the next day. She replied asking him to consider leaving her alone for good. Sire would not give up easily, however. He wrote Sandy a poem, filled with misspelled words and elementary grammar. Sire was a great talker, but his writing skills were comparable to a fourth grader. His true talent was mastering numbers. The poem did its job. It just so happened that Sandy had a weakness for poetry. She invited Sire over to her apartment for thanksgiving, which was only a week away. Sire knew that he had a decision to make. He had to leave Kezzie alone for good.

The air was cold and dry outside. Sire was sitting in the back of a grey Gypsy cab on route to Sandy's place in Bushwick. On the seat near him, was a bag with a bottle of white wine, and another with pumpkin pie which he had purchased at the supermarket near his residence. It was his contribution to Sandy's Thanksgiving dinner. The apartment was nearly full by the time Sire arrived. Most of the people there were close family and friends of Sandy's, including her parents who Sire met for the first time. One look at Sandy's father and Sire could tell where Sandy's Indian side came from. He was a short dark-skinned man with straight black hair. Her mother was slightly taller than her father. She was a curvy, brown-skinned woman with short hair. The dining table was packed with a plethora of Guyanese and American dishes. On a small table in the corner of the dining room, there were sodas and a variety of alcoholic beverages. Sire poured himself some wine and went to sit on the couch next to Sandy's cousins. Shortly after, Sandy introduced him to the rest of the family. They were all very welcoming. Before the night was over, Sire would feel like he was a part of the family.

December was usually a slow month for car dealerships. Around that time, people spent most of their money on Christmas presents and new furniture. Things usually picked up again around tax season. Sire used the slow season to organize his database and keep track of sale patterns. Since Thanksgiving, his fling with Sandy had evolved into a relationship. They spoke more often and visited each other intermittently. Sire tried to avoid temptation by staying away from Kezzie. He told her that he was moving on with his life and did not wish to see her again. He would soon realize, however, that Kezzie wasn't an easy girl to get rid of. One evening, Sire received a phone call from Kezzie's aunt. Sire had met her while he and Kezzie were still dating. Her name was Lisa. She was having a birthday party at her place for her sister, and she wanted Sire to DJ for her. Against his better judgment, Sire accepted the job, knowing that there was a strong possibility that he would run into Kezzie. She had been living with Lisa for the past year.

On the day of the party, Sire arrived at Lisa's house around 6pm. Kezzie was in the kitchen looking after the food. She was wearing a red Eileen Fisher dress that fell right above her knees. She glanced over her shoulders and saw Sire talking to Lisa in the living room. Sire avoided the kitchen and headed to the basement to set up the sound system. The birthday girl arrived shortly after, while the rest of the family showed up gradually. Before long, Lisa's house was packed to capacity. Sire searched for music that suited the mature crowd. He had become a master at selecting, a sort of skill that was acquired with years of being a DJ. By midnight, most of the guests had left and it was time for Sire to pack his things. Lisa was getting sleepy, so she left some food on the dining room table for Sire, before retiring to her bedroom upstairs. Moments after Sire sat down to eat, Kezzie took out a plate of food for herself and sat directly across from him. The two of them locked eyes briefly. It was a quiet scene, except for the clattering of the cutlery on the plates. Suddenly, they locked eyes across the table. It was as if in that moment, they could read each other's mind. The food was quickly forgotten as they both rose from the table, embraced, and began to undress one another. They ended up on the living room couch, not caring how much noise they were making. After it was all over, Sire went back to his place with a heavy weight on his heart. It was the weight of regret.

New York was finally getting a break from a brutal winter. March signaled the beginning of spring and with that came the sight of new prospects. Sire had completed a few songs throughout the winter, and he was trying to put a project together. One afternoon, he was at the dealership sipping some coffee when he got the phone call that would change his life for good. Sandy had just left the doctor's office and was informed that she was three months pregnant. There's a lot that goes through a man's mind when he receives an "I'm pregnant" phone call. Sire imagined getting such a phone call from Kezzie, and he almost lost his bearings. He was delighted that it came from Sandy, but nervous about the changes to come. Sandy, on the other hand, was concerned about how Sire would receive the news.

"What do you want to do?" She asked him.

"We are keeping it," he said.

"Okay you don't seem surprised."

"I had a feeling."

"Why? Because I gained weight?"

"That, and the fact that you ate up all my snacks."

"Shut up. I kind of had a feeling since I missed my period."

"Hmmm. And you did not say anything."

"I wanted to be sure."

The cab driver dropped Sire off in front of the E-Building. The time seemed to have flown by since Sandy confirmed her pregnancy. Nine months was hardly adequate time to prepare for a baby. As he got out of the taxi, Sire wondered what was so special about the number nine that made God decide it was appropriate for baby making. It was only his second time coming to Kings County Hospital. His first visit there was due to food poisoning. Even then, the only reason he went was because he was throwing up at work, and Eva forced him into her car and drove him to the ER. This time he was there to witness the birth of his child. The automatic doors opened as he walked towards the entrance. There was a female security guard standing behind a large desk. The area seemed rather uneventful for a hospital lobby. There were two ladies dressed in blue scrubs, chatting near an elevator. Sire walked up to the security guard and told her that his girlfriend was having a baby and he was not sure what floor he was supposed to be on. The baby was not due for another few weeks, but Sire had gotten a call from Sandy's sister. She told him that she had brought Sandy to the hospital after she began having contractions. The security guard took Sire's ID and gave him a visitor's pass to stick on his shirt. "Sixth floor," she said passively before handing Sire his ID back.

Sire took the elevator up to the sixth floor. As soon as the doors opened, he saw Sandy's mother and sister speaking with one of the nurses. When Sandy's sister saw him, she yelled out "the baby is here!" Sire walked up towards the three of them with a curious look on his face. "Is this the dad?" The nurse asked. "Come this way." She gestured for Sire to follow her through the corridor and led him to a private room where Sandy laid on a bed with the baby in her hands. There was another nurse in the room who looked like she was running diagnostic tests on Sandy and the baby. Sandy's face lit up as she saw Sire walk into the room. She looked like she had just lost a fight with a hair blower. Sire kissed her on the forehead. He took one look at the baby boy and suddenly there was nothing in the world that meant more to him. He reluctantly took him in his arms, like he was afraid of dropping him. "Welcome to the world Andrew," he said.

Sire walked down the squeaky wooden steps in the apartment to let Kezzie in. As they walked back to the room, he noticed that the steps were noisier than usual that night. Then again, every sound seemed to be amplified after midnight while most people were already asleep, he thought. It was a quiet night and Sire was in the mood for some action after spending hours playing with his home studio. It had been a month since Andrew was born and he hadn't been able to find the time for sex lately. He spent a lot of time with Andrew whenever he was not working. At the time, he hadn't yet told Kezzie that he had a son. After an hour of intense sex, Sire regained some of his objective senses. It was time for him to tell Kezzie the truth. Kezzie was lying next to him, distracted by something on her phone. "I have a son," he said. Kezzie paused what she was doing for a moment, looked at Sire blankly, and then turned back to her phone. "How old is he?" She uttered, almost uninterestedly. Kezzie's nonchalance to the news wasn't a complete surprise to Sire. She was a very strategic woman. Her silence only meant that there was something cooking inside. "He's a month old," Sire replied plainly. A few weeks later, Sire received a disturbing text from Sandy. "Who is Kezzie and why is she reaching out to me on Facebook?" She asked.

## CHAPTER 7

Sire had just woken from a dream when he saw Sandy's message. Somehow, he was not surprised by it. Kezzie had been quiet since he revealed that he had a son. He found it odd and assumed that she was up to something. Sandy's text message confirmed it. Kezzie wanted to wreak havoc and she knew where to start. The message was short, but it was enough to cause a stir. It read "how well do you know Sire?" Sandy's intuition led her to assume that Sire was having an affair with Kezzie. Still, she wanted to give Sire the chance to explain himself. His response was succinct. "She's just some girl I used to deal with. Don't respond to her," he said. He looked at the time and realized that he was running late for work. After a quick shower, Sire was on his way. By the time he arrived, there were two customers waiting for him to assist them. He apologized for being late and went straight to work. Once he had some free time, Sire checked his phone and saw four missed calls from Sandy. He scratched his head nervously before returning the call. Something told him that Sandy had taken Kezzie's bait.

"Let me guess," Sire said with a sigh. "You spoke to that girl, right?"

"So, is it true?" Sandy's tone was direct and stern.

"It depends. I don't know what this crazy girl told you."

"You were sleeping with this woman behind my back for over a year."

"She was just a distraction"

Before this unfolded, Sire had considered telling Sandy about the affair. However, he became reluctant when Sandy got pregnant. She was clearly hurt by this discovery, but Sire offered little words of reassurance. The conversation continued with Sandy spewing insults towards him. He absorbed everything she told him, like a sponge. It went on for a few minutes until Sandy struck a nerve. She called him a "deadbeat" father. That was when Sire lost his composure and exploded. The thought of someone labeling him a "deadbeat" made him sick. It hit twice as hard coming from Sandy. He always strived to be a good father. Sire let off some steam and then promptly ended the call.

It felt like any other day at the job. The only odd thing was the scattered snow flurries in the sky. The temperature outside seemed rather warm for there to be any sign of snow. Sire was outside in the lot talking to a potential buyer when he saw someone strolling past the dealership from the corner of his eyes. He glanced to his left and saw a young lady looking in his direction. Sire had become familiar with most of the regular passersby, and he was sure he had never seen her before. With light brown skin and thick hair, she appeared to be a mixed chic. She had a petite figure, but her shape was attractive like one of an athlete's. Sire felt like he needed a distraction since his argument with Sandy. Since that day, he avoided speaking with her unless it pertained to his son Andrew. He fixed his mouth to say hello to the young lady, but no words would come out. It was the true definition of being speechless. The young lady, as if amused by Sire's staring, gave a slight smile and continued along her way.

For the remainder of the day, Sire could not get the mystery woman out of his head. He imagined her smiling back at him as he stared into the darkness of his room. "I'll call her Monalisa," he whispered to himself as his eyes became heavy with sleep. The following day he was determined to see her again. Around the same time as the day before, Sire went out to the lot hoping to catch the mystery woman walking by. To kill some time, he began washing some of the cars. It took him back to the days when he had just entered the car dealership business. He had come a long way since then. At that moment he remembered Shawn and felt guilty for not keeping in touch with him more often. Shawn had given him the start which led him to the position he was currently in. Sire reached for a rag near a Honda Civic he was cleaning when he turned and saw the mystery woman staring directly at him. For a second, he froze, as if he were under a spell. He threw the rag in a bucket nearby and went to greet her out on the sidewalk.

"Hello," he said. "You look familiar."

"Hey, I remember seeing you yesterday. You work at this dealership right."

"Yes, I'm the manager here. I saw you looking at one of the cars. Or maybe you were looking at me?"

The young lady laughed. "No, I was wondering why you were staring at me like that."

Sire blushed. "My name is Sire. What's yours."

"Ella."

Sire strolled alongside Ella until they reached the end of the block. "So, you live around here?" He asked.

"Yes, I live a few blocks up."

"Okay. I don't think I have a business card on me." Sire patted his pockets even though he knew that he never had any business cards in the first place. "Take my number," he said. "In case you're ever looking for a car."

For the next few weeks, Sire and Ella would become close acquaintances, talking on the phone intermittently. Ella was born in Haiti. She moved to New York with her mother at age fifteen after losing her father three years prior. Her mother found a job as a nanny and was able to put her through school. Ella graduated from high school and obtained an Associate's degree from Kingsborough Community College. Although she had no legal papers, Ella was able to work because of the Dream Act which was introduced by the Obama Administration. On her way home one afternoon, Ella met Sire at the dealership, and he walked her to her apartment building. She turned to Sire and planted a kiss on his mouth before reaching for her keys in her purse. Sire followed through like he was expecting it. The relationship quickly evolved into a sexual affair. Ella wasn't perturbed by Sire's relationship with Sandy. She was only there for a good time.

Sire wanted to set the mood for the night. He didn't bother to buy wine because Ella did not drink alcohol. It was his first time dating a woman who neither smoked nor drank. Instead, he went to the supermarket and bought some snacks in case she got hungry. When Ella arrived, the first thing that she noticed was the makeshift home studio. She asked Sire to play her a couple of his songs and just like that, she became his number one fan. Just as she was getting comfortable, Ella noticed one of Andrew's bibs on Sire's futon. It had a picture of a purple dinosaur on it which resembled Barney. Andrew had left it there the night before while spending time with his dad. Ella picked up the bib and studied it.

"How old did you said your son was again?" She asked.

"He just turned six months."

"Wow, and he's your first. You must be a proud dad." Ella put the bib back down on the futon near where she sat. Her body language had shifted slightly, signaling some guilt. Sire noticed her discomfort and reassured her with a kiss. While they were kissing, she told Sire to pull her tights off, revealing a red see-through thong. That was enough to get Sire excited. Ella had an electrifying sexual energy that Sire hadn't felt in a long time. It was like losing his virginity all over again.

On Wednesday night at approximately 8pm, Sire and Ella went to Stumpy's Jamaican Cuisine for some food, chicken soup for Sire and curried goat meal for Ella. It soon became a weekly routine, and the server quickly became accustomed to their regular visits. She would greet them with a smile and ask if they wanted the usual. After collecting their food, they would proceed to the corner store across the street. Sire would pick up a two-liter bottle of ginger ale and a fresh pack of black and mild cigarettes. He admired the fact that Ella did not judge him for his habits. She was raised in a strict household and church was a major part of her upbringing. One day, she got into a huge argument with her mother for sleeping out at Sire's place. Sire did not realize it at the time, but he was beginning to fall for Ella in a way that he never could have imagined.

A beam of dawn's sunlight peered through the window. A drop of dribble fell onto Sire's pillow as he snored. He dreamt that he was driving down King's highway when his phone began to ring. It was somewhere in the car, but he just couldn't find it. He began reaching under the seat to search for the phone and woke up to find it ringing next to his pillow. He wiped the froth from the crease of his mouth and picked the phone up. It was Sandy. He had forgotten about their arrangement. Sandy had planned to go on a road trip with a few of her friends that Sunday, and she told Sire that she would drop Andrew off at dawn. He answered the phone, let off a grunt, and proceeded to drag himself down the steps to collect Andrew. It took a few seconds for his eyes to adjust to the sunlight when he opened the door. The first thing he noticed was how beautiful Sandy looked. It had been quite some time since the two were intimate. Sire wondered if he could get a quick one before she left, but Andrew was wide awake, and it would have been almost impossible to keep him distracted.

Nevertheless, Sire was happy to see his son and looked forward to spending the day with him.

The following week, Ella and Sire were walking home from the restaurant when they became engaged in a discussion regarding natural hair. Sire stated that he preferred seeing women in their natural hair rather than weaves, adding that he found women in weaves to be quite undesirable. Ella, who would wear the occasional weave every now and again, felt offended and uttered "well at least white boys like it." Baffled by Ella's remarks, Sire stopped for a second and asked Ella to explain what she meant. She walked away, seemingly embarrassed by the comment, and Sire decided not to press the issue. The following week, the couple were hanging out at Sire's place after having dinner. Sire was on his laptop downloading beats from YouTube, while Ella laid on the bed scrolling through her social media. Sire wanted Ella's opinion on a particular beat he had found. He tried getting her attention, but she seemed distracted by something on her phone. It was only after he called her name for the third time that she responded. She hopped off the bed and walked over to Sire to apologize, placing her phone down near his laptop. Sire happened to look down at the phone which revealed a picture of a Caucasian man wearing a blue t-shirt with a guitar in his hands. He picked up the phone for a closer look.

"Who's this?" He asked.

"He's a friend."

"Friend? A friend got you so distracted that you can't even hear me calling you?"

Ella stood up straight, like she was addressing a judge. "I was just checking to see if his eyes were blue or green," she said.

"What the….." Sire paused for a second. There was an odd feeling stirring in the pit of his stomach. It was a feeling that could break a grown man: when you suspect that the woman you love was falling for someone else.

A few weeks had gone by, and things were back to normal for the two lovers. Sire's insecurities had dissolved, and he felt like he had Ella's attention again. The music had begun to thrive as well. Sire released a Soca song that was getting a lot of recognition, so Ella created a fan page for him. By this time, Sire referred to himself as an artist rather than a DJ, despite Milo's criticism of his singing. His gradual move away from the DJ business almost put a rift between him and Milo, but he had made up his mind about what he wanted to pursue. One evening, after practicing some vocals, Sire received a disturbing phone call from Ella. She had just finished having a nasty argument with her mother. According to Ella, her mother had been trying to convince her to marry someone in order to obtain a green card. He was the nephew of the lady she was working for, who happened to be Caucasian. One day, Ella's mother showed him a picture of her, and he became entranced by her beauty. Since that day, he persistently asked Ella's mother to introduce him to her, promising to help her with her green card. Sire's first instinct was to try calming Ella down. He understood that he was in no position to help her with a green card and that it would be selfish of him to prevent her from obtaining one with someone else. Sire told Ella to get some rest, and that they would discuss the matter in the morning.

It was the first time the couple had been out to eat, diverting from the usual Jamaican take out. Sire thought that Ella could use some cheering up, so he invited her out to Applebee's for lunch. He arrived a few minutes late and noticed Ella sitting in the waiting area wearing a pink dress. She did not immediately see when Sire arrived, sitting with an emotionless look on her face. Sire walked up to her and laid a kiss on her forehead, and her mood seemed to change slightly. They were seated near a clear window. The waitress was dressed all in black with a red apron around her waist. She handed them the menu and told them that she would return to take their order. Ella stared out the window. Sire held her hands as if he were going to propose.

"Hey, cheer up," he said. "What's the matter?"

"I'm not going to marry him."

"If you don't feel comfortable doing it then fine. But don't let it be because of me. I'm not in a position to provide this kind of opportunity for you."

"It's not only that. There's more."

"Well?"

Ella looked at Sire, and then looked away again. "My mother wants me to stop seeing you," she said.

"So what? She can't stop us from seeing each other. We know what we have."

"You don't understand. She threatened to do voodoo on you and your son if we don't stop."

Sire let go of Ella's hand and leaned back in his seat. The waitress approached the table with a pen and notebook in hand to take their order. "Give us a few more minutes please," he said. Sire looked up at the ceiling, as if searching for some guidance. He wondered why someone would threaten to harm an innocent child, his own flesh and blood. He thought about paying Ella's mother a visit but knew it would not end well. He turned to look at Ella again. "Don't worry about my son," he said. "He will be just fine."

"I just don't know what to do," Ella replied.

Sire signaled for the waiter. "We're just gonna grab a few drinks at the bar. Here's a tip for your time anyway."

Sire laid on his bed staring at the ceiling. It was quieter than usual at the apartment. There was no noise coming from the neighboring rooms. First-responder sirens had seemed to disappear for a while. He hadn't seen Ella in over a week. They hadn't spoken much after their date at Applebee's, but it was Thursday and Ella had promised to sleep over that night. Sire waited for her until his eyes became heavy, and he fell asleep. The next morning, he jumped out of his sleep. Ella never showed up. It was almost time for work, but somehow, he could not find the strength to get up and prepare himself. He sent a message to Eva advising her that he was not able to work that day. Sire reached for a cigarette in his pants pocket but remembered that he had smoked the last one the night before. He flung the pants away in frustration. There were no missed calls or messages on his phone from Ella. Sire began to reminisce. Just a month prior, he was the happiest man in Brooklyn. How could things have changed so drastically, he wondered. His mind drifted back to Ella's mother and what she had said about his son. Suddenly, Sire jumped out of bed and proceeded to put on his clothes. It was time to pay her a visit.

The fog outside was unusually heavy, and the air was dry and cold. The walk to Ella's house was at least thirty minutes. This gave Sire a lot of time to think about what he was going to say to her mother. He realized that he had never heard Ella say her name. She usually referred to her as "Ma." However, it did not matter at that point. He was hurt and he wanted to hurt her for forcing Ella away from him and threatening his son. Sire made a left turn onto Ella's block. His rage seemed to intensify the closer he got to her house. Just as he was pushing the front gate open, he felt his phone vibrate. He reached for it in his pocket and saw a picture of Ella lying down in what looked like a hospital bed. He immediately called her phone. She told him that she wasn't feeling well so she checked herself into a hospital. Sire tried to get the name of the hospital from Ella, but she would not give it to him. She simply said that she was going to be fine, before ending the call. Sire forgot all about Ella's mom and went searching for the nearest hospital, which was Brookdale. After giving the receptionist Ella's full name, he was told that no one had been admitted by that name, so he went home.

A few days had passed since Sire had last spoken to Ella. He was just about to fall asleep when he heard a knock on his room door. He assumed it was one of his roommates. Surprisingly, it was Ella. The last time they spoke, she was still at the hospital. She was the last person that Sire expected to see standing in front of his door. He wanted to be angry with her; he was, for abandoning him. Ella scanned the room as she walked in, like a new habitat. Sire grabbed a t-shirt from one of his drawers.

"So you're alive." He said plainly.

"I've been very stressed lately. It has taken a toll on my health."

"What are you so stressed about?"

Ella took her jacket off and sat on the chair next to Sire's computer desk. "With all that's been going on," she said. "I'm getting married in two weeks."

"So that's why you disappeared. Look, I already told you from before, I know I can't help you. But that doesn't mean you have to ditch me like I never meant anything to you."

"I know, I'm hurting too. It's just.......... complicated."

Sire wiped his face with his hands. He felt bad for not considering Ella's feelings in all this. After all, she was the one who was marrying a stranger for God's sake. "Do whatever you have to," he said. "Just don't treat me like an outsider."

After a few weeks, Ella was officially a married woman. Since their last meeting, Sire would speak to her intermittently, but it was only through scattered text messages. After her wedding date had passed, Sire noticed that all of Ella's social media accounts had become inactive. He tried calling her on a few occasions, but it seemed like her phone had been disconnected for some time. Sire became confused and depressed. He couldn't understand how someone who claimed to love him so much could just abandon him with such ease. At times, he wondered if she was held against her will or if her evil mother had made some type of deal and sold her off as a concubine. He contemplated going to Ella's house, but he did not want to risk being labeled a desperate ex or a stalker. He just wanted to know that she was alive and safe. Eventually, he turned to alcohol to drown his sorrows when it became evident that he wasn't going to get Ella back. One night, Sire's phone notified him that Ella had posted a picture on her Instagram. It was a picture of her and a Caucasian man on what seemed to be a cruise ship. Ella was wearing shorts and a straw hat. She seemed happy, angelic almost. She was sitting on the man's lap. The man was wearing shorts with a plain white t-shirt. Sire studied his face. He looked very familiar. He took a closer look and realized something. It was the same man that he had caught Ella staring at on her phone. It was a damning realization. It led Sire to question everything that she had told him about her situation with her mother. She had fallen in love with the Caucasian man, and she needed a way out. Sire proceeded to block Ella on all his social media accounts. He put on some clothes and made his way down the street to Stumpy's Jamaican Cuisine. He ordered the usual before heading to the corner store.

Sandy finished cleaning the kitchen, then brought Andrew into the room to comb his hair. Sire sat at the dining table, struggling to remove the bones from the brown stewed red snapper he was feasting on. He took no pleasure in eating certain foods where the work overshadowed the reward, like bony fish or crab. Sandy's father had prepared the fish. It was one of his specialty dishes. He noticed Sire struggling with it and chuckled.

"You didn't eat a lot of fish growing up boy," he said.

"No, not really. We ate lamb."

Sandy's father pulled out a chair and sat across from Sire. "Where you from again? Zambia?"

"Nigeria, but my family moved around a lot."

"Sometimes I wonder why we leave our good homes to come to this country and work like slaves. I had a whole house back home in Guyana son. Huge house." He opened his hands wide to indicate the size of the house. "Now I'm here living in this small apartment, and I can barely stretch my leg without bumping into something."

"True." Sire nodded.

"But you know why I did it son?" His facial expression tightened. "It was for the children. To give them a chance at becoming something great. Its already too late for me. I'm in my fifties. I shouldn't have to work this hard just to keep a roof over my head. But in life son, we have to make sacrifices."

"That's true."

"When do you plan on marrying my daughter son?"

Sire's eyes opened wide, like he was witnessing a live robbery. "Well, we haven't really spoken about it as yet."

"So what are you waiting for son. You already have a kid with her. You're a step ahead. All you have to do is tie the knot. You do love my daughter, right son?"

"Of course, I would do anything for her."

"Okay son, I know you'll do the right thing. You're a good man."

Sire retreated to Sandy's bedroom after he finished eating. Sandy was still combing Andrew's hair. She was amused when Sire told her about the conversation he had with her father. There had been a few occasions where her father had asked her if Sire was planning to marry her. However, she never imagined he would ask Sire directly. "He must have had a few drinks," she said. Prior to Andrew's birth, Sire could not envision himself walking down the aisle. He wondered why any man would want to willfully commit themselves to one woman. However, his outlook on marriage had changed since Andrew's birth. He knew it was the best move to make for his family, but he struggled with commitment. It had been three months since Ella ejected herself from his life. The first month was the worst. Ella's scent remained on his pillows. He felt lost, helpless and struggled to focus on anything else but how he was feeling. Now, he was almost back to his normal self, paying more attention to his family and his music.

His relationship with Sandy became stronger with time. She grew to accept him for who he was, whether he was faithful to her or not. He was a good father and she valued that over anything else.

While they were speaking, Sire got a call from Milo, but he did not answer. Sire had noticed things about Milo that did not sit right with him. The two of them had not spoken in months due to several incidents that occurred in the past. The first incident occurred at a deli on Saratoga Avenue and Newport Street. Sire and Milo entered the deli to buy some beer, when they noticed someone familiar. His name was Mega, a well-known gangster from the neighborhood. Mega gestured Sire over to speak with him. Sire did not know Mega personally but would see him from time to time in the neighborhood. Although he was known for being a gangster, Mega had spent a lot of time in prison and had begun to reform his life since he was last released. He knew that a lot of young men in his neighborhood glorified the gang lifestyle and he wanted that to change. Mega participated in community meetings and events, urging the youth not to be tempted by the effulgence of drugs, money and crime. Sire and Mega would pass each other often when Sire visited the deli, giving each other a nod when making eye contact. He noticed Sire's calm demeanor compared to the other young men in the area and told him to remain positive and to keep his head up. While paying for his items, Milo saw the two men speaking and decided to approach them. "Hey man, why you speaking to that fake rasta," Milo said. He tried to pass it off as a joke, but Sire knew that it came from a place of jealousy. From that day he began keeping a slight distance from Milo. However, it was not until an incident occurred between Milo and Sire's ex Kezzie that he decided to completely distance himself. He had received a call from Kiezzie's cousin warning him that he needed to watch his friends. When asked to elaborate, she told him that one afternoon while video chatting with Kezzie she noticed that Kezzie was at Milo's place in what looked like his bedroom. When Sire confronted Kezzie with the news, she simply stated that she was only there for DJ lessons. In that moment Sire realized that Milo was not the friend that he had originally thought him to be.

The following day, while working Sire realized that he hadn't seen or spoken to Shawn in quite some time, so he gave him a call. Shawn was happy to hear from him. He was pleased at how quickly Sire was able to move up in the dealership business.

"You're the true definition of a hustler," he said. "Just a year ago you were washing cars. Now you're managing a whole dealership."

"Couldn't have done it without your help. I'll always be grateful. How's thing over there on your side," Sire replied.

"Things were slow for some time, but it's starting to pick up. Just a while ago I was coming from the coffee shop, and I met two sexy girls right outside the dealership. I think one of them is Jamaican. Her name is Jackie or Janette or something. I don't know but she's gorgeous. The other one is nice too. She's from around your area. You know Shay?"

"Brown skin tone with the pretty face?" Sire asked.

"Yes that's the one. She's cute but I have my eyes on the friend. She's tall and dark-skinned and she has a banging body. They told me that they wanted to hang out this weekend. I'll probably call you if I need a wing man."

"I hate to turn down a good time, but I'm trying to turn over a new leaf. I'll probably be spending time with the family," Sire responded.

"When did you decide to finally grow up? I respect it though, for real. I for one will not be joining you anytime soon. I'll probably call Milo to see if he's free."

On Sunday, Shawn called Sire to catch him up on what had taken place over the weekend. He told him that he had invited the girls and Milo over to his place for drinks. It was raining that day and the girls arrived around 10pm. Shawn was interested in Jackie, so he tried to hook Milo up with Shay. However, things didn't go as planned because Milo wanted Jackie and not Shay. Shawn told Sire that Milo tried to impress Jackie with stories of his thrilling lifestyle as a DJ and brought up Sire's name several times. Shawn reported feeling annoyed with Milo but tried to hide it. His plan had backfired, and he regretted involving Milo in the first place. Despite both men vying for her attention however, none got lucky that night. Sire chuckled while listening to the story and thought to himself *'typical Milo,'* but did not say it aloud.

The following weekend, Sire was having some drinks at a local bar when he received a call from Shawn. The music at the bar was quite overbearing, so he went outside to take the call. Shawn was on his way to a birthday party in Queens together with Jackie and Shay, and he wanted to know if Sire would tag along. Despite turning down Shawn's invite just a week prior, Sire had some liquor in his system, so he was up for some action. A few minutes later, Shawn arrived in front of the bar in his white Range Rover and told Sire to jump in the back next to Shay. Jackie was sitting in the front passenger seat. As he was driving off, Shawn decided to break the ice. "Shay, you remember Sire, right?" He asked. "Yes of course I remember him," Shay responded. "He doesn't know how to keep in touch with people." Sire blushed. "Well hello Shay, it's been a while" he replied. Before Shay could respond, Shawn turned to Sire and said "this beautiful young lady sitting next to me is Jackie. She's my soon-to-be wife." Jackie rolled her eyes. "Since when?" She asked. Sire found the exchange amusing. "Well Shawn, you have your hands full," he said. Shawn was low on gas, so he stopped at a gas station along the route to fill the tank. As soon as he stepped out the vehicle, Jackie turned around to face Sire.

"So, you're the famous Sire huh?" She asked.

"I didn't know I was famous," Sire replied.

"Well, I've heard quite a lot about you from your friend Milo."

"Oh boy. Well, I hope he didn't scare you."

"Far from it."

"Well, I would not get too excited if I were you. Milo likes to exaggerate sometimes."

Just as Shawn reentered the vehicle, Jackie ended the conversation and turned back around. They arrived at the party at around midnight. However, shortly after arriving a fight broke out which led to the party ending early. Just outside the venue, the four of them ran into some friends who were mutual friends of Sire and Shawn. Someone from that group suggested a club in Brooklyn called Tracks, so they all decided to go check it out. On the way to Brooklyn, the other vehicle got into a fender bender on the highway, so they pulled over in the service lane to wait for the police to arrive. An hour later, there was still no sign of the police arriving. By this time, everyone had exited the vehicles and they were blasting music as onlookers drove past them. While this was happening, Sire caught Jackie staring at him a few times, but avoided making eye contact with her because he did not want to upset Shawn. Still, he found it difficult to resist the lure of Jackie's beauty. By the time the police arrived, it was almost five in the morning. Tracks was closed by then, so they decided to go the Arch Diner for breakfast instead.

If you were from Brooklyn and enjoyed the nightlife, at some point you would have ended up at the Arch Diner. It was where revelers went to fill their liquor-filled stomachs with food before retreating to their homes. The diner was packed by the time the large group arrived. Luckily, a polite waitress was able to pull two tables together for them to sit. Shawn made sure that Jackie was seated next to him, while Sire and Shay sat across from them. It did not take long for Shay to notice Jackie's attempts to get Sire's attention. She found it quite amusing. Rather than waiting around for the waitress, Shawn decided that he was going to order at the counter. He asked Jackie what she wanted so that he could pay for her food. As soon as he left the table, Jackie focused her attention on Sire.

"So...... what are you getting?" She asked.

Sire flipped through the pages in the menu. "Uh.... I'm not too big on breakfast, but I'm definitely hungry."

"Do you want me to choose for you?"

"Sure, surprise me."

Jackie headed to the counter to order Sire's food. Meanwhile, Shawn was heading back to the table with their order. He assumed that Jackie had gone to pick up napkins from the counter. To his surprise, Jackie returned to the table with a plate filled with French toast and scrambled eggs and placed it in front of Sire. Shawn could not believe what he was seeing. He had just paid for this woman's meal, and she thanked him by paying for another man's meal right in front of him. Shay found the whole ordeal quite amusing and desperately tried to stifle her laugh. Sire, on the other hand, felt a little embarrassed for Shawn. The last thing he wanted to do was to offend him, but Jackie had put him in a tough spot. The ride home was quiet and awkward. Shay was dropped off first, and then Sire. As he was getting out of the vehicle, Jackie turned towards him as if to say something, but she was quickly interrupted by Shawn. Sire noticed what was happening, so he made his exit swiftly.

A few days after that eventful night out, Sire was having lunch at the dealership when he received a text message from Shay. She told him that Jackie would not stop mentioning his name. Before he had time to respond, Shay sent him Jackie's phone number. He reluctantly saved the number, knowing that he would be tempted to cheat on Sandy again. Later that night, while unwinding to some music after work, Sire dialed Jackie's number. The conversation was brief. She did not sound very excited to hear his voice. Sire was slightly confused by this, but he played it cool. That Friday, Sire received a rare phone call from Milo. It was the first time they had spoken in months. Milo was going to an event hosted by a mutual friend and wanted to know if Sire was up for it. Sire rarely said no to a night out unless he was sick.

He told Milo to pick him up in an hour. Milo arrived just after 10p.m. As the two men drove off, Milo told Sire that he had to pick up someone on the way. He drove for a few minutes, and then pulled over in front of a three-story apartment building. Sire assumed that it was one of Milo's cousins. He sometimes joked with Milo that half of Brooklyn was related to him. Sire peered through the dark tints and saw someone in the shape of a woman approaching the car. She opened the rear passenger door behind Milo. "Goodnight boys," she said. To Sire's surprise, it was Jackie.

The trio arrived at the event just before midnight. It was held at a ballroom in Long Island. The dress code was semi-formal, but jeans and sneakers were not rejected. Jackie wore a long Cashmere turtleneck dress. A classy look, compared to the two men, who were slightly underdressed. They entered the event together, like a celebrity and her two-man security team. Sire kept a safe distance away from Jackie, because he was unsure if there was something going on between her and Milo. All he knew was that they had met previously, and if he knew Milo, he was trying to get Jackie's attention one way or another. The ballroom was decorated with balloons and confetti, like a high school prom dance. Sire and Milo were familiar with the DJ. They would have been glad to play a few tunes if they were asked. It was a DJ's instinct. After greeting the DJ, the trio headed towards the bar where they were met by some old friends and acquaintances. It only took two glasses of Moscato for Jackie to become tipsy, and then she latched on to Sire like a seatbelt. Sire tried to remain poised, but it wasn't long until Jackie's appeal got the best of him. He turned to her and caressed her while they slow danced to the music. Meanwhile, Milo met up with an old girlfriend who kept him busy for the night. Her name was Rhonda. They had met at a wedding a few years prior. When the event was over, Milo convinced Rhonda to catch a ride home with them. They arrived at Sire's place first. He invited Jackie in, but she stated that she had to work in the morning. Milo suggested she retrieve her uniform from her house so that she could spend the night at Sire's. Sire was shocked that Milo spoke on his behalf. Nevertheless, Jackie obliged.

Sire took the bag from Jackie's hand and placed it on the computer chair. "Where do you work?" He asked.

"I work at IHOP. Why, do you have a job for me?"

Jackie sat on the bed and pulled her panties out from under her dress, keeping her eyes focused on Sire's face.

"As a matter of fact, I do." Sire unbuckled his pants and let them drop to his feet.

"Are you sure you can satisfy my wages sir?" Jackie leaned back on the bed with her dress still on and spread her legs open. Sire took off the rest of his clothes and situated himself between Jackie's legs.

"I'm sure we can come to some type of agreement," he said.

The sex lasted until dawn. It was almost time for Jackie to get ready for work, but she decided to call out sick instead. Sire had a few hours to spare before it was time for him to leave for work. It was a good opportunity he thought, to discover what laid beneath the beautiful face and attractive body.

Jackie was born and raised in St. Ann's Bay Jamaica. She was the third child of her mother, who had four children by four different men. Her father tried his best to be a part of her life, up until his untimely death when Jackie was only six years old. After being reported missing for three weeks, his body was discovered in a marsh near his home, with what appeared to be stab wounds to his chest. It was rumored that his death was payback for a murder he had committed a few years prior, but he had never been officially charged with the crime. Jackie's mother struggled to provide for her four children. Her only source of income came from selling bread and pastries to villagers nearby. When Jackie turned thirteen, she connected with one of her aunts on her father's side via social media. Her name was Shirley. She was living in New York at the time, and she encouraged Jackie's mother to apply for a visa for her. She even sent money to help with the fees. As soon as Jackie obtained her visa, she migrated to New York to live with Shirley in Queens. Shirley put Jackie through school, where she excelled with good grades. However, her dreams of going to college were halted when she became pregnant shortly after graduating from high school. The child's father was young and wanted no part of his child's life, stating that Jackie had been sleeping with other men while they were together. Jackie decided against taking him to court and opted to raise her child on her own. A few years later, Jackie met a gentleman who was five years her senior. They dated for some time and then decided to get married after Jackie became pregnant with her second child. Overtime, Jackie's husband grew madly in love with her, but she could not reciprocate that love back. Nevertheless, he provided her with a green card and financial security, so she stayed with him. One day, he discovered that Jackie had been unfaithful to him, so he filed for a divorce. Since then, Jackie has been focused on providing for her two kids, but sometimes found herself entangled in fruitless relationships. Sire was marveled by Jackie's openness. Over the next few months, they developed a bond. They were similar in many ways, but they each had a mystifying trait that the other admired. At times, Sire found himself craving Jackie's presence. It was becoming an addiction. Jackie's promiscuous nature had little effect on his feelings for her. If anything, he found it arousing. The relationship between the two had become rather publicized after they had been spotted out at numerous events.

Sire was part of a WhatsApp group chat consisting of a group of DJs and a few old friends, male and female. Most of the group members were Guyanese, and they were all connected in one form or another. The guys enjoyed nothing more than to have a crack at each other, and nothing was off limits. One morning, Sire woke up to a slew of messages from the group. He scrolled through the chat and found a picture of Jackie resting comfortably in bed with another man, posted by none other than Milo. At first, Sire assumed that it was an old picture which Milo had found on one of Jackie's social media accounts, but a date stamp proved otherwise. The picture was taken the previous week. Before leaving home for work, Sire reminded himself that Jackie was merely a temporary distraction. Still, there was an unsettling feeling in the pit of his stomach. He looked at the picture again. The date was exactly one week from the present day. He replayed the events of that week in his head. There was nothing odd about it except for a shift change at Jackie's job. There was no sudden change in behavior, nor were there any nasty fights or arguments between the two. Sire could not find any reason why Jackie would seek comfort in the arms of another man and could still find the gall to take a picture of it. By this time, he was halfway to work, not even realizing that he had skipped his usual stop at the deli. After contemplating, Sire hesitated slightly before forwarding the picture to Jackie's phone. Exactly seventeen seconds later, his phone started to ring.

"Where you got that picture from?" Jackie asked.

"Doesn't matter where I got it. It matters who's in it," Sire replied.

"It was a mistake. I shouldn't have, I...... It just happened."

"And you let him post a picture of you."

"I didn't know he was going to do that. I would have stopped him."

"Well, it doesn't matter now. I gotta get to work."

The rest of the day was quiet, somber almost. By nightfall Sire had begun to erase the image of Jackie from his memory. The picture did not serve its intended purpose. If anything, it made Jackie more desirable, like a forbidden fruit. That night, they had passionate sex. It was the best that Sire had gotten in quite some time. The next morning, Sire was sure that he had been bewitched. Jackie's scent followed him everywhere he went. Around that time, he had begun to have suspicions that Milo was trying to sleep with Jackie behind his back. He had caught wind of a rumor that Jackie and Milo had been spotted out together at various events. Up until the picture incident, Sire had chosen to ignore the rumors, but he couldn't afford to let Milo get one up on him.

A few weeks later, Sire told Jackie that she needed to stay away from Milo, but she insisted that they were merely friends. One morning, an argument ensued between the two. They exchanged a few disrespectful words before hanging the phone up on one another. It was the first time that a disagreement between them had reached that level of disrespect. That night, Sire received an odd phone call from Milo. The call started off casually, about music mostly, and then the question came. "So, what's up with you and Jackie?" Milo inquired. Sire's response was an emotional one. He said some things about Jackie that he did not mean. What he didn't know, however, was that Jackie had heard every word of it. She was sitting in Milo's car while he had the phone on speaker. After the call ended, Milo drove Jackie to his place where they had sex on his living room floor.

It was a quiet Sunday afternoon. Sire was reading a book to Andrew while Sandy twisted his locks. It was days like these that kept Sire grounded. At times, he imagined a devoted lifestyle, free of temptation and lust. Infidelity was a full-time job and it had begun to take its toll. Still, there was a part of him that was drawn to the lure of novelty, like a creature of habit. Andrew fell asleep after only four pages of reading. It was a children's book written by Bill Martin named "Brown Bear." Sire had bought it for him one afternoon while he was shopping at Target. As he got up to put Andrew down on his bed, a text message came in from Jackie's cousin Gayle. *What now*, he thought. Gayle had just turned thirty, so she was hosting a small party just outside of her apartment in Bed-Stuyvesant. Sire had met Gayle while he was still dating Jackie. He thought it was odd for her to invite him since he and Jackie had not spoken in some time. Surely, Jackie must have told her something, he wondered. However, nothing was mentioned regarding Jackie or any arguments of the sort. At the time, Sire knew nothing of Milo's interference in his fallout with Jackie. Milo had dated Gayle in the past, but they did not end on good terms. After putting Andrew to bed, Sire told Gayle that he would be at her place in an hour.

Sire arrived on Gayle's block just after 9pm. Some distance away from the house, he could make out a few people from the crowd. A blue Pelle Pelle jacket was all he had to see to know that Milo was there. He was the last person that Sire expected to see at Gayle's party. He began walking in Milo's direction but was spotted by Gayle, who ran up to him and gave him a hug in the middle of the block.

"Come with me to the corner store," she said. "We need more ice."

"Gayle, I haven't seen you in forever. Happy birthday."

"Thanks, hun. You're the one who's been staying away."

"I've just been working hard lately."

"I hear that. What's the deal with you and Jackie? I'm hearing she's messing with your boy now."

"Who, Milo?"

"Who else? I confronted her about it, but she hung the phone up on me. I mean that's just foul. I would never date one of her exes. She knew me and him had our history."

Sire held the door open for Gayle as they arrived at the corner store. A black and white cat followed them to the back of the store where the freezer was.

"Well, I heard a rumor about it, but I'm as clueless as you. I haven't spoken to her in some time. We had a little falling out, so she can do as she pleases," Sire said, while pulling three bags of ice from the freezer.

"It must be true. Otherwise, she would have come to the party. Milo and I are cool now, like I don't have any grudges. He's actually at the party right now."

"Yea, I saw the jacket."

"So are you guys cool."

"We bump heads all the time. But we never fell out over Jackie. I mean at this point; I don't really care to be honest."

"Yea, I feel you. I'm still upset with Jackie though."

"Gayle, do you still want the man?"

"Of course not."

"So then just let them be."

They returned to the house with the ice and Sire greeted some of his familiars, including Milo, who did not stay too long after Sire arrived. By the end of the night, Sire was inebriated. The news about Jackie and Milo had affected him more than he wanted to show, so he tried to stifle his emotions with alcohol.

The following day, Sire sat at the office discussing his afflictions with Eva. She had become accustomed to his poor choices in women and had summed them up to a lack of maturity. She was in a 10-yearlong committed relationship with a man that used to date her aunt, so she functioned more like a pair of ears rather than a judge. After noticing how Ella's betrayal had affected Sire, Eva had hoped that he would have turned over a new leaf. He had previously mentioned wanting to give up the unsettling lifestyle. After hearing about Jackie, Eva had given up hope. Still, Sire liked sharing his stories with her. He found it to be therapeutic. A few hours before closing time, Sire received a text from Jackie asking him to stop by after work.

Sire had been to Jackie's apartment many times before. There was an eerie feeling in the air as he followed her through the hallway that led to her door. She was wearing black biker shorts and a white t-shirt. Once inside, Sire looked around to gauge his surroundings. He was slightly anxious and thought he might be walking into and ambush with Jackie and Milo. Instead, He was greeted by Jackie's two sons, who were watching television from the living room couch. They were both quite familiar with him. They had grown accustomed to seeing a male face around the house from time to time, although Jackie tried to keep that part of her life away from them. She gestured to Sire to follow her into the kitchen.

"Anything to drink?" She asked.

"Anything that's not poison," he replied.

"I would never, you know that. I think I've done enough harm already."

"So, it's true then. You and Milo are a thing now."

Jackie opened the fridge and pulled out a Heineken. "Yes, it's true," she said.

"So what am I doing here?"

"I wanted to apologize……. in person."

"A text would have been fine."

Jackie opened the Heineken bottle and handed it to Sire. "I just don't want us to be enemies, but I'll understand if you want to stay away."

"Listen, you've made your choice." Sire took a sip of Heineken. He got a slight brain freeze when it hit the back of his throat. "I won't burden my heart with hate. I'm good."

Sire stood up to leave but Jackie obstructed his path. She grabbed his left hand and slipped it into her shorts.

"So you don't miss this?" She asked.

Sire tried to resist the temptation. His mind screamed no, but his flesh was erect. Jackie brought him to her room where she performed a strip tease for him. Sire helped her to remove the last article of clothing and proceeded to undress himself.

Satoshi Kanazawa, an American-born British psychologist once said that men do everything they do in order to get laid. Therefore, women will always have more power than men. Sire hardly doubted the validity of that statement. For the next few months, he was content with Jackie being a "friend with benefits," while she was supposedly in a committed relationship with Milo. "Modest payback" he called it, after all what Milo had done to him. One afternoon, Sire and Jackie were having intercourse while Milo was calling Jackie's phone. Without warning, Sire pressed the answer button and gave the phone to Jackie. He had an empowering feeling watching Jackie try to stifle her moan. Her responses were short and direct. Sire thrusted faster and deeper until Jackie hung up the phone abruptly.

Experience had taught Sire to savor the good times because they did not last very long. He was taken aback one morning when Jackie called and explained that Milo wanted to have a baby. She went on to say that they had already begun trying. She asked if he would be alright with this new change as if seeking approval. At first, Sire laughed at the absurdity of what he was hearing, but soon realized that Jackie was being serious.

"So you're really doing this?" He asked.

"Yes, I've been thinking about it for some time now."

"Of all people. What happens if he finds out you're still sleeping with me. You think he's gonna stay with you? Jackie, think about this for a second. Forget about me. Milo is not a reliable man."

"Yes, but he really wants to build a life with me. He deserves a chance."

"Then go ahead, if that's what you really want."

Even after their conversation, Sire was sure that Jackie would eventually come to her senses. He could not envision Milo taking care of Jackie and three kids. He also had his own selfish motives for not wanting Milo to get Jackie pregnant. He had a good thing going and a baby would surely mess everything up for him. The fun would stop sooner than Sire had anticipated, however. Just two days after that conversation, he received a stern message from Jackie. She wanted to be left alone so that she could focus on her relationship.

After procrastinating for some time, Sire finally brought his coats to the dry cleaners so that he could store them away for next winter. It was only the first week in May, but the warm summer air had already begun to knock on the door. Marlon was gearing up to launch his annual family fun day celebration at Seaview

Park in Canarsie. Sire was considered family, so he didn't need an invitation. Every year, he made it his duty to make an appearance. Things had been quiet for him since Jackie had asked him to leave her alone five months prior. Seaview Park was usually crowded on a typical Sunday in May. Around that time, Brooklyn residents were eager for some outdoor activities after hibernating during the winter. Marlon's family was situated on the East side of the park near the basketball courts. Sire arrived a few hours late as he did every year, just in time for the liquor. Alcohol was not permitted at the park, but if there was one thing West Indians were good at, it was hiding liquor. As he entered the park, Sire noticed an aroma of jerk chicken in the air. Marlon's uncle was on the grill. He had taken over from Miss Ingrid after complaining that she was burning the chicken. There were children chasing after a soccer ball that looked like it needed air, but they enjoyed kicking it around. Marlon had brought a small generator to power up the speaker so that he could play music for the family.

The event was well attended by family members and friends, most of whom Sire was familiar with. It didn't take long for him to find the liquor at the bottom of the cooler. By the time the sun had begun to set, he was stumbling from drunkenness. Marlon asked him to help pack up the equipment in the vehicle but noticed that Sire could barely stand on his own. He asked one of their mutual friends to give Sire a ride home. His name was Kelvin. However, instead of giving Kelvin his address, he gave him Jackie's. He had a sudden urge to see her but wasn't quite sure what he was going to say. It wasn't until he was standing in front of Jackie's building that he realized how ridiculous he looked, so he made a U-turn and began to walk towards his apartment. While he was walking, Sire decided to go on Snap Chat to see what Jackie had been up to. He had stayed off social media for quite some time, but on that day, he was feeling exceedingly curious. Sire scrolled through Jackie's pictures attentively. She seemed to have put on some weight, almost unrecognizably in some pictures. There was one picture that stood out. Jackie was wearing a long white maternal dress with a "it's a girl" caption underneath the picture. Her stomach looked bigger, protruding through the dress almost. Sire stopped and stared at the picture for a minute with his mouth wide open, before going inside to his room.

Seeing Jackie in a maternity dress had a sobering effect on Sire. He phoned a few of his friends in the area to find out if there were any rumors going around regarding Jackie's pregnancy. He could not ignore the possibility that the baby could be his. Disappointingly, all the phone calls he made turned out futile. Everyone he had spoken to either knew nothing of Jackie's pregnancy, or they had just assumed that the baby was Milo's. There was only one thing left to do. He dialed Jackie's number.

"Hello stranger," she answered.

There was a slight pause, and then Sire said "No, I think you're the real stranger."

"Oh my, don't say that. You know I still love you."

"Do you even know what that word means?"

"Of course I do, and I know you love me back. That's why you called; you couldn't stay away from me any longer. Am I wrong?"

"Yes, you're wrong. I called because I accidentally came across a recent picture of yours. First off, I want to say congratulations. Secondly, I just want to know if it's mine."

There were sounds of plates clattering in Jackie's background. "Why don't you come over and I'll tell you. Milo is out of town."

Sire had read something in a magazine about pregnant women having elevated sex drives, so he knew better than to take the bait. "Look, I don't want to come over there. I just want to know if it's mine," he said.

"It's not," Jackie answered plainly.

"You're sure?"

"You sound disappointed."

"I'm just trying to do the responsible thing, but I wish you all the best. Anyways, let me not keep you too long. It was nice talking to you."

A few months had gone by, and Sire had gradually begun to fall back into his regular habits. He visited the liquor store more frequently and spent more time locked up in his room making music. By then, he was gearing up to release his first album. Jackie had given birth to a beautiful baby girl. Sire had gotten a few glimpses of the baby from social media posts. There were moments when he looked at the baby and saw similarities to his son, Andrew. Ultimately, he decided to rest the issue and let Milo and his family have their peace. Besides, his birthday was only a few days away and he did not want to encourage any bad energy around him. Sire had been speaking to Richie about potential locations for him to celebrate. Richie had since settled his differences with Milo, and they were back on talking terms. He had also reconnected with a long-time girlfriend after she sent him a friend request on Facebook. Her name was Karishma. Sire was quite familiar with her. He had seen her out with Richie on various occasions, but at the time he did not know that the two of them were in a relationship. She was born and raised in Brooklyn, but her parents were Guyanese. She normally kept her hair short which complemented her curvy figure, with two large breasts that looked like floating devices. Her exuberant personality was just as captivating as her cleavage.

After some deliberation, Sire decided that he would celebrate his birthday in Williamsburg, at a club called Bembe. Sire and Richie had been to Bembe many times before. They appreciated the diverse crowd of partygoers who frequented there. Richie sent out a message on the group chat with details on the address and time. Most of the group members showed up, along with some other mutual friends. Richie was surprised to see Sire without a female companion that night. What he didn't know however, was that Sire had a secret affair with one of the women in the chat room, an older woman named Sue. She was a married woman who had been sneaking around with Sire ever since he and Jackie had stopped speaking. Sue was forty-five, but she looked ten years younger. She was dark-skinned and pretty with a petite body size. Her old-fashioned glasses made her look like an elementary school teacher. Sue's husband was in his sixties. They had two kids who were entering college. Sire knew that she did not have any deep emotions for him but instead was just seeking a little thrill outside of her mundane 20-year marriage. She had made it clear from the beginning that she loved her husband and even admitted at times to feeling guilty after having sex. However, the excitement of it all kept her coming back.

That night, Sue kept her distance from Sire, trying not to arouse suspicions from the other group members. They had already made arrangements for her to spend the night at his place. Sue told her husband that she was spending the night at her sister's house to avoid driving back all the way to Long Island. At the end of the night, Richie offered Sire a ride home, but he declined and told him that Sue was dropping him off on her way to Long Island. Sire was eager to get home. The taboo nature of this type of romance added extra excitement to the intimacy. Once inside, the couple began to undress each other in the hallway, as if there was no one else living there.

Sue was the first to wake the next morning. She had set her alarm for 8:30am. It was Sunday and she wanted to get home in time to cook lunch for her husband and kids. Sire was in a deep sleep at that time, snoring even. Sue watched him for a few seconds as she put on the extra panty that she had kept in her purse. She kissed him on his forehead and left the apartment. By the time Sire woke up, it was midday. He noticed that Sue was gone. He sat up on the bed and looked around for his phone. It was time for him to go see his family. He took a shower and headed to Sandy's place, where he spent the rest of the day.

The next morning, Sire woke up to a number of "happy birthday" messages. One of them stood out. It was a message from Karishma on his Snap Chat account, which read "happy birthday Lion King." Only one person ever called him that name. "Tell Jackie I said thank you," he replied. Moments later, Sire's phone started ringing. It was none other than Jackie.

"What a surprise," he said.

"Happy birthday lion king, did you miss your queen?"

"My queen huh? She's in Nigeria somewhere taking care of my siblings."

"I hear you birthday boy. So, what do you have planned for the day?"

"Nothing, besides work."

"I heard about your little party on Saturday. You could have invited me."

"I assumed you had mommy duties, and since when did you and Karishma become besties anyway?"

"Richie introduced us. I think he was trying to get me to do a threesome with them, but I'm too smart for that. She's cool though. I like her."

"Yea, they've been on and off for some time now."

"Just like us, right?"

"I think we're more off than on."

Jackie laughed. "That can be fixed. Let me come and give you something to make up for that."

"Come see me after work," Sire replied after a slight hesitation.

CHAPTER 10

It's been said that you really don't know someone until you've lived with them. Jackie came to believe this to be true after only three months of living with Milo. He had been living with his mother after getting evicted from his place but decided to move in with Jackie shortly after their daughter was born. Aside from Milo's intermittent party gigs, Jackie was the sole income earner. Milo stayed home with the baby, while the boys went to school. This left Jackie with some freedom for her extracurricular activities. However, Milo's idleness soon manifested into insecurity, while Jackie grew frustrated under the pressure of supporting the family on her own. There was a side of Milo that Jackie had not seen until recent. For one, Milo had a strange sense of entitlement which Jackie despised. He refused to look for a regular job yet expected Jackie to come home to clean and cook. As time went on, Jackie began to regret having a relationship with Milo, but she was happy for her daughter and did not want her to grow up without a father like her boys. Whenever Jackie felt like the pressure was mounting up, she turned to Sire for relief.

One evening, while venting to Sire about Milo, Jackie mentioned that Richie had suddenly taken up interest in her. Sire knew that Richie was an opportunist where sex was concerned. The first time that Richie met Jackie, she was sitting in Sire's room with denim shorts and a tank top. Richie had stopped by to drop off a pair of speakers. Sire could tell that Richie was attracted to Jackie by the way he looked at her. From that day on, Sire knew that Richie would have seized any opportunity to sleep with Jackie. When Richie found out that Jackie had dumped Sire for Milo, he suddenly decided that it was time for him and Milo to settle their differences. As he spent more time around Milo, he took the opportunity to get close to Jackie in an attempt to sleep with her behind Milo's back. Jackie explained that one afternoon, after hearing her say that she enjoyed watching lesbian porn, Richie told her that he knew someone who was into girls, and he wanted Jackie to meet her. "That's when he first mentioned Karishma," she said. The two girls eventually met at a barbeque one afternoon. Jackie told Sire that she was drawn to Karishma's bold personality. Sire shook his head while listening to Jackie's story. Despite knowing Richie's tendencies, he was marveled at how calculated he was to use Karishma to bait Jackie into having a threesome with him. Richie would be disappointed, however, because his plan failed to work despite Jackie and Karishma becoming close friends.

A few weeks later, Richie added Sire and the girls to a chatroom. At first, Sire did not find it odd because they all knew each other. However, he would soon realize that Richie had another plan in the works. After finding out that Jackie was seeing Sire behind Milo's back, Richie figured that he would have a better chance at sleeping with Jackie if he went through Sire. Richie's motives mattered little to Sire. He always thought that chatrooms were more entertaining than television. They usually came with all the amenities you would expect from your favorite television series- drama, comedy, action, to name a few. This one was just more intimate. Richie suggested that that the four of them should meet up for drinks some time and everyone agreed. All that was left for them to do was for them to pick a location.

The day before they were set to go out for drinks, the group decided that they would hang out at Sire's place instead. The decision came after a week's long discussion on group sex. What was first meant to be an innocent double date soon turned into a full-on orgy. The girls seemed to be enthusiastic about the idea, but Richie was the master mind of the operation. The day had finally arrived. Sire left work early so that he could get his place ready for the grand event. That usually involved getting rid of the clutter of clothes and empty liquor bottles from the floor and couch. As soon as he made it up the stairs of the apartment, Sire noticed a strong marijuana smell coming from the room next door. The room belonged to a St. Lucian man who had moved in about six months prior. His name was Winston. He was a tall, dark-skinned man with a bald head and a beard that covered half his face. Winston hardly ever said much and usually kept to himself, unlike the other roommates. He had a son around the same age as Sire's, who stayed with him for one weekend out of the month. It was the first time that Sire had ever noticed a marijuana scent coming from Winston's room. He did not come off as the smoking type. His head was always shaved clean, and his beard neatly lined up. He dressed in office attire for work, shirt and tie, although Sire wasn't sure what his profession was. Sire assumed that Winston may have had a friend over that night, but then again, even college professors smoked marijuana, he thought. He took his phone out of his coat pocket and dialed Richie's number to ask what time they were going to show up.

Sire's phone started ringing around 11pm. Richie had arrived downstairs with the girls, and they were eager to escape the boisterous cold wind. Sire answered the door bare-chested, only wearing a pair of sweatpants. He had drunk a sip of rum moments earlier, so he felt immune to the elements for a short time. The four of them made their way up the narrow staircase leading up to Sire's room. The marijuana scent from Winston's room had faded. Sire wasted no time stripping down to his underwear once they were inside. There was a slight hesitance among the others, like onlookers at a party waiting for someone to start dancing so that they could join. The girls hung their jacket up behind the door while Richie reached for some liquor. Both girls were wearing dresses beneath their coats. Jackie wore a grey sheath wool-knitted dress and Karishma wore a black fitted one. Sire was amused by Richie's apparent nervousness. He found it funny since Richie had been the most vocal in the chatroom. Even the girls seemed more relaxed than him. Without delaying further, Sire took Jackie by the hand and led her to the bed. Jackie was ready. At that moment in time, Sire was her king and all she wanted was to pleasure and satisfy him, even if it meant opening herself up to another. She took off her dress, revealing her naked body and then climbed on top of him. Karishma followed suit, grabbing Richie by his belt before undressing him. She then threw him on the couch next to the bed before getting on top of him. They were beginning to get aroused as they watched Sire and Jackie in action. Just as Sire and Jackie were about to change positions, Sire uttered "switch," and then went over to Karishma while Richie got his chance with Jackie. It almost happened too fast for Richie. There was little time to savor the moment. As he penetrated Jackie in missionary position, he felt a disconnect. Jackie's attention was fixed on Sire, like she was having sex with him vicariously.

The following day, the chatroom was unusually quiet. Sire woke up to an empty bedroom, which resembled the aftermath of a swingers' party. He nearly fell over an empty bottle of Gin as he got out of bed. While brushing his teeth, he thought about the events that took place the previous night and wondered if there was more to life than just satisfying carnal desires. Then a thought came to his head. He wondered if he could ever change his lifestyle. The allure of the bachelor's life had begun to fade. He remembered a conversation he had with Sandy's father during dinner some months prior. What seemed to be just another awkward conversation at that time was now a subject of interest. As he walked back to his room, he heard his phone vibrating near his laptop. It was Jackie.

"Thought you were still sleeping," he said.

"I wish. The kids woke me up to make them breakfast."

"The joys of motherhood."

"It's a gift and a curse, but I love them to death. You're getting ready for work?"

"Yes, my room is a mess. Next time we're getting a hotel room."

"Next time? I don't know if I can do that again. I mean it was something new. I liked the excitement, but watching you make love to Karishma like that was like torture. It was like an out of body experience, you know. I barely felt anything from Richie, my body was numb, and my spirit was absent. I guess I was just selfish."

"Damn, was I that good?" Sire chuckled. He found Jackie's cathartic confessions quite amusing, although he vaguely remembered feeling Jackie's eyes on him for what seemed like a long period of time. "Well next time I'll take it easy," he said.

"Don't flatter yourself Sire."

Before leaving for work, Sire looked back at his messy room, like he was about to embark on a long journey. He knew that it would look the same when he returned from work, but he wanted the image to stick in his brain. He wanted a new start.

A few months had gone by, and Sire had begun to turn over a new leaf. He started looking around for an affordable apartment with plans on getting his family under one roof. It would mark an initial step in the right direction, but first he had to tie up some loose ends. Sire had been trying to distance himself from Jackie for the past few weeks, but she was relentless. One evening, she showed up at his place unannounced demanding an explanation for his absence, but Sire pretended to be exhausted from work and told her that he would call her in the morning. The following day, Sire decided to pay Jackie a visit after work. Milo was booked for a gig in New Jersey, so he thought he had a few hours before Milo returned to the house. He had only planned on being there for a few minutes. When Sire arrived, Jackie was holding the baby in her arms while the two older kids were sitting in the living room watching cartoons. It was his first time seeing the baby in person, still wondering whether he was her real father or not. Sire sat on the couch next to the kids. There was a sound of a whistling kettle coming from the kitchen, which prompted Jackie to turn the stove off. She proceeded to prepare the baby's bottle. Sire was amazed at how much the two older kids had grown. They were both old enough to understand that Sire and their mother were not together anymore, but he wasn't sure if they knew that he wasn't supposed to be there. However, it did not matter much to him at that time. He had come to set the record straight with Jackie, and finally move on with his life. He walked over to the kitchen where Jackie was, but before he could begin speaking, Jackie's phone rang. It was Milo. For what seemed to be a moment, Jackie was silent after she answered the phone, and then she abruptly headed to the living room window and peeked outside. Sire could tell that something was up by the look on Jackie's face. Before he had time to ask a question, Jackie ran back into the kitchen and mouthed the words "he's here." There was no time to hesitate. Sire could hear keys rattling outside the door. "Quick, go to Phillip's room," said Jackie. "Hide in the closet." To Sire's surprise, the little boy saw what was happening and came to escort him to his room. Upon entering the room, Sire noticed that Phillip's room was not like the typical boy's room. The bed was neatly done, there were no dirty socks or old toys on the floor, and the walls were spotless, void of any crayon marks or cartoon posters. Towards the back of the room, there was a door that was left slightly open. "In here," Phillip said, while pointing to the door. It was a small walk-in closet, consisting of winter coats and other articles of clothing. Sire fitted himself in between the winter coats and sat on top of a plastic container, leaving him exposed from the legs down.

Although Phillip had closed his room door, Sire could faintly hear Milo speaking with Jackie in the living room. He had been in the closet for approximately twenty-five minutes. Each time Sire heard someone's footsteps, his heart rate sped up a little faster. He thought about sending a text message to Jackie and remembered that he had forgotten to put his phone on silent. Luckily no one had called him yet. Meanwhile, Jackie was trying to get Milo to leave the apartment. She told him that she was feeling extremely nauseous and that she needed some Pepto-Bismol from the pharmacy. However, Milo was uninterested and told her to use the bathroom or boil some tea. He became suspicious when Jackie persisted. After almost an hour of hiding in the closet, Sire heard Phillip's room door open for a few seconds, and then close back again. His heart nearly skipped a beat. He wasn't afraid of Milo, but he knew not to underestimate the unpredictability of a hurt man. Milo had scanned Phillip's room for a few seconds before closing back the door. Still, he got the feeling that something was off.

Sire had officially been trapped in the closet for two hours. He received a text message from Jackie which read "He's not leaving. I think he suspects." By then, Jackie and Milo had retired to their bedroom together with the baby. Phillip, seeing that the coast was clear, decided to check on Sire. Hearing the door open again, Sire tried to make himself smaller. He listened to the footsteps as Phillip approached the closet. Anxiousness turned into relief when he saw Phillip's face. Phillip gave Sire a thumbs up and closed back the closet door before exiting the room. Sire could only shake his head in amazement; he had always liked the kid.

In the other room, Jackie was waiting for Milo to fall asleep so that she could assist in Sire's escape. She had assumed that Milo's suspicions were quelled after he seemingly became comfortable. She was mistaken, however. The moment she went to use the bathroom, Milo reentered Phillip's room. He knelt to look under the bed. Sire peeped through the crease of the door and saw Milo kneeling near the bed, like a Muslim in the midst of prayer. He knew it was only a matter of time before his cover was blown. Milo approached the closet and opened it with caution. He knew that something was off by the way the coats were slightly bulging out, not noticing Sire's exposed feet. Using his hands, he spread the coats apart and all he could see was Sire's face staring back at him from the darkness. Milo lunged backwards in fright, landing on his backside. Sire was so amused by Milo's display that he let off a slight chuckle, disregarding the gravity of the situation that he was in. After hearing the chuckle, Milo jumped to his feet and went for a closer look, revealing Sire's grinning face.

The night Sire and Milo met they could not have imagined how their friendship would have played out. They certainly could not have envisioned their current state of affairs; Sire hiding in Phillip's closet and Milo fishing him out. The shock of seeing Sire's chalk-white teeth emerging from the darkness of the closet left Milo speechless. The only word he was able to utter was "wow." Sire, on the other hand, could not contain himself. The look on Milo's face sent him in a laughing frenzy. By then, Jackie was aware that Sire had been found and she was just hanging out in the living room awaiting the outcome. The commotion had awoken the baby who had just fallen asleep. Everything was unfolding like scenes from a TV drama. Milo was distraught, but he had to compose himself to save face. "Jackie, come in here!" he yelled. "Come get ya man." Jackie was not ready to deal with that situation. She walked past Phillip's room and went to pick up the crying baby. Milo was not going to let up so easily. He stomped into the other room demanding an explanation from Jackie, while

Sire tried his best to calm things down. He offered to talk, but Milo wanted Jackie to remain in the spotlight as he bombarded her with verbal attacks. Things took a turn for the worst when Milo asked Jackie if Sire was the baby's biological father. That's when Jackie lost all her composure. She laid the baby down in her crib and immediately began to throw Milo's clothes out of the bedroom while shouting "I want you out of my place." Sire tried to intervene, but Jackie could not be stopped. She wanted Milo out of her sight. No one seemed to care that the baby was still crying, so Phillip picked her up and gave her to Sire. Things had gotten so out of hand that Milo had to call his friend Will who lived nearby to help him pack up his stuff. When he arrived at the apartment, the first thing he noticed was Sire holding the baby. Will had been privy to the love triangle among the three, so one can only imagine the look on his face when he walked in. It was at that very moment Sire realized something. Neither Jackie nor Milo wanted to leave. It was Sire's presence that was fueling the already volatile situation. Once the baby was settled and stopped crying, he handed her over to Jackie and made his escape.

A few months later, Sire was doing his laundry when he received one of the most important calls of his life from a close friend and business partner. His name was Leslie. They had met through a mutual friend and had been working on music together for approximately one year. Leslie was one of the few people who saw great potential in Sire's singing ability. Not only was he a writer, but he was also a smart businessman. Together, the two friends had created a collection of Reggae songs worthy of an album. Leslie told Sire that that an award-winning producer had heard a few of his songs and wanted to collaborate with him on his first studio album. Sire did not know it at the time, but it would mark the beginning of a flourishing musical career. Things were looking up for him. Sandy was pregnant with their second baby, and they had recently secured a lease for a two-bedroom apartment in Williamsburg a month prior. He hadn't seen or spoken to Jackie in months, and he no longer felt the urge to mix and mingle with other women. After the call, Sire stood there for a few seconds with the phone in his hand and smiled. He was finally doing right by his lady, and he was being blessed in return with this new opportunity. Sire glanced up at the ceiling and silently thanked God and made a promise not to ever return to his old ways. He looked back down with a smirk on his face and exited the laundry with his clothes.

One evening, Sandy took Sire out for dinner to celebrate his achievements. They were seated at a long table with extra chairs. Sandy told Sire that she wanted to surprise him, so she invited some of his friends. A few moments after they sat down, Sandy's phone rang. She told Sire to give her a second while she collects the guests at the door. Sire was shocked to see Sandy returning to the table with Jackie walking behind her. They were followed by Ella, Kezzie, Heather, Denise and lastly, Deborah. All seven ladies sat down at the same time, each of them smiling graciously at Sire. He looked around the restaurant and noticed that everyone else had left. Then he looked back at the ladies, studying each of their faces intently. Still, none of them said a word. He heard Sandy's phone ringing again. It kept ringing and ringing until he finally woke up. It was all a dream. He turned to Sandy lying next to him and asked her to put her phone on vibrate.

# EPILOGUE

Approximately one year after moving to Williamsburg, Sire was walking home from work one evening when he thought he heard someone say his name. He glanced over his shoulder but did not see anyone that he recognized and continued walking. Moments later he felt a hand tapping his shoulder. Sire's heart nearly skipped a beat when he turned around and saw Ella smiling back at him. It was as if he was seeing a ghost. "Hi," said Ella while maintaining her smile. She appeared amused by Sire's facial expression. "Ella?" Sire replied. Without saying another word, she pulled Sire into a hug, and he hugged her back. She asked what he was doing in the neighborhood, and he explained that he had moved there recently. The two of them walked down the block casually while they spoke. Neither of them seemed to be in a hurry. Ella told Sire that she moved to Williamsburg with her husband shortly after they got married. She apologized for exiting his life the way she did but explained that there were things in play that were beyond her control. Sire wanted to ask whether the story she had told him regarding her mother was true, but he decided against it. Ella told him that one day she would explain everything to him. They walked for a few more blocks and then Ella told him that she had to stop at the supermarket to get groceries. She hugged Sire one last time and then continued down Morgan Avenue.

Printed in the United States
by Baker & Taylor Publisher Services